THE MAN WHO
OWNED THE EARTH

THE MAN WHO OWNED THE EARTH

A.K. VIJAYAKUMAR

PARTRIDGE
A Penguin Company

Partridge books may be ordered through booksellers or by contacting:

Partridge India
Penguin Books India Pvt.Ltd
11, Community Centre, Panchsheel Park, New Delhi 110017
India
www.partridgepublishing.com
Phone: 000.800.10062.62

CONTENTS

To
J, R and C, for all the times we went to those magic
casements opening on the foam of perilous seas
in faery lands forlorn

FOREWORD

Much of the story takes place in present day Northwest India. It has become necessary, therefore, to import occasional words from the vernacular, or draw from the culture and mythology of the region. Consequently, I have appended a glossary for those who may be unfamiliar with such terms or references.

PROLOGUE

From the morning of all time comes a fable of a king and his rash promise . . .

Many they were, who came unto his great Yagna . . . They came from the far corners of an ancient land . . . Kings and Queens . . . Princes and potentates . . . The learned and the wise . . . They came to look and wonder . . . From the snow clad loftiness of distant mountains came sages and seers . . . "To behold the ceremony is to be blessed", they said . . . It is said that the Gods themselves descended to the Earth to bear witness.

And at the end of it all, to those assembled spake thus the King . . . "None among those who have honoured this great ceremony with their presence shall leave with any desire unfulfilled", he said. . . . "Ask and whatever ye desire, it shall be given to thee" . . .

And through a long day the King gave and gave till his arms were weary and a grateful throng went away, praising the King and blessing him for his generosity . . .

And at the last came a slight looking figure of a Brahmin boy. Of him the king queried thus gravely, hiding his smile. "What might be your desire, my son?"

"As much land sire, as three paces of mine can compass", replied the boy. "Take it then", said the King. "It is thine".

With his first step Vamana took in all of Earth . . . And with his second, all Heaven . . . And then did he pause to look enquiringly at the King . . .

There is, however, a story somewhere about a later king . . .

CHAPTER 1

THE GUEST

The car glided uphill smoothly, its headlights probing the darkness with twin lances of light. Presently it had reached the first street lights of the little village. "Macholi", the driver said, pointing ahead with a little stab of his forefinger before his face. The lone occupant in the rear seat nodded uncertainly. Through the smudged and dust-caked window, he could see above him a spread of lights, with bright little lines strung out along ascending private roads that led to houses. It was a luminous gossamer against the velvet darkness of the mountainside. The car stopped now and the driver got out to enquire. He got back and started the car. It crept forward slowly as the driver craned his neck out, looking for the landmark that would signal the point where he would have to leave the road. He found it presently and stopped the car to inspect the mud path that had been cut out of the hillside. It was a steeply rising ramp of tamped-down earth, with clumps of coarse grass growing through it here and there. The vehicle now began to whine up the gradient and after a five hundred meter progress, reached the house and stopped.

The man who got out of the rear seat was obviously a foreigner. While he cautiously unfolded his tall frame segment by segment from the cramping confines of the car, the driver carried his leather valise, placed it outside the door and rung the bell. When the door was opened by a servant, the two men conferred briefly before the latter vanished into the house carrying the passenger's grip. Within a minute he had returned with a man who was evidently the owner of the house. The newcomer saw a small-built individual with a bustling air about him.

"I'm Viswanath Prasad", the latter announced as he shook the other's hand. "My brother spoke to me about you, professor Steinhardt".

"Bruce", said his interlocutor with a smile. "Your brother was most helpful. And I think it a piece of colossal luck that I learned about you. I can't quite believe it, in fact". Steinhardt paid the driver and followed his host into the house, stooping a bit under the lintel of the doorway. He found himself in a well lit room in which a large table had been placed, with a couple of chairs around it. A divan and two heavier wooden chairs completed the furniture of the room. Prasad waved his guest into the former now and pulled up one of the chairs to sit down facing his companion.

Under the lamplight, Bruce Steinhardt was a big man. It was a rugged, rawboned bigness that had 'Outdoor' stamped all over it. The lines and deep furrows on his cheeks and the pepper-and-salt stubble on it made him appear a good ten years older than his forty five years. By contrast, there was a plump and jovial, almost Dickensian rubicundity about his companion that suggested a character out of Pickwick Papers. So that, in spite of a thinning crop of hair, his sixty years sat lightly on him and he looked no older than his visitor. There was a moment's silence while Steinhardt unzipped his valise, drew out a wallet and checked the papers in it. He then settled himself comfortably in his chair and then looked at his host.

"I'm told you are a mathematician and are interested in the mythology and folk tales of this region. It's a rather unusual combination of interests, if you may permit me to say so", said Prasad.

Steinhardt chewed his underlip thoughtfully. "That's right", he said finally. "In mathematics, I work in something called number theory and there are people I know who can, and do, think about nothing else for months on end. You see, you've got to be what a friend of mine once described as a twenty-four hour man if you want to do good work in this field. But . . . .", Steinhardt voice tailed off as the servant brought in a tray with two glasses of water on it. He took one of the glasses, nodded his thanks to the bearer and tossed off the contents, almost as if to get that ceremony out of the way. He dabbed his lips lightly with a handkerchief and waited for his host to finish drinking the water. "But, you know, this kind of work can take a terrific toll on you." Steinhardt stopped and stared musingly for a moment before continuing. "Most mathematicians like myself, who aren't in the first rank, have some other interest which allows one to get away now and then. It's an effective way to preserving your sanity. And, oddly enough, these secondary interests are sometimes quite often compelling in their own way".

"But tell me about yourself", he continued. "I understand you share my interests".

The older man nodded. "I'm by training a botanist. After retiring from college teaching last year, I've devoted myself to the work I've always dreamed of doing. My family's in Delhi and they don't think much of this place. All this is tribal area, you see", Prasad waved a hand vaguely and paused. "There's nothing much happening in Lahaul-Spiti. And I don't mind living alone. Once in three or four months, I go to Delhi and spend a few weeks there".

The other man nodded. "You're doing some work here?", he enquired.

"I'm writing a book on the herbs growing here. This is also a wonderful place to study the birds of Himalayas. And finally, of course, there's the mythology and folklore of the region". Prasad stopped to glance at the clock. "It's eight, now. If we finish dinner, we can sit outside and have our talk. I'll see how much of your questions I can answer. We can start at around midnight for the temple".

"Won't that be a bit late?", asked Steinhardt. "I wouldn't like to miss anything, if I can help it".

"No, no" said Prasad quickly. "He never starts before midnight and the place is barely five minutes from here by car. Come, I'll show you". He walked to the window and threw it open. When Steinhardt joined him, he could see the moonlight pouring over a grassy knoll that he estimated to be about half a mile away. Prasad pointed to the top of the swell. "Can you see the temple?", he asked. By straining his eyes Steinhardt could just make out the tiny white spot on top, which would have been invisible in anything less than the flood of silver radiance that bathed the knoll.

"Can we go all the way to the top by car?", he asked.

The other shook his head. "We can reach the foot of it and then climb up around hundred steps".

He turned to his guest. "I was not sure what sort of dinner would suit you. Since I didn't know how to make an American dinner . . . ." Prasad looked uncertainly at Steinhardt as they made their way back to the chair.

The younger man leaned back in his chair and grinned at his host. "This is my fourth trip to India Prasad *Ji*. I wouldn't be here now if I wasn't entirely comfortable with this country and its ways. Especially in the matter of food. I'd however prefer a light dinner. And less spices the better".

"You don't have to worry about that ", said Prasad and got up. He went inside and returned in a few minutes. Presently the servant entered, carrying two trays. He placed these on the table and withdrew, to reappear with a jug of water and two glasses. The mathematician pulled up a chair to the table and sat down. When he removed a white cloth covering the tray nearest him, the fragrance of curry assailed him. Prasad sat on the opposite side and uncovered his tray. There was a bowl of fruit and a plate on which were a couple of little bottles, which Steinhardt knew to be seasoning used commonly with fruit dishes. "I take only fruits at night for dinner", said Prasad, by way of explanation.

Dinner was a brief affair, with the two men finishing it in almost complete silence, each busy with his own thoughts. After it was over, when the plates had been cleared away, they carried their chairs outside to the lawn. The moon was a huge blazingly incandescent disc now, hanging low in the sky. On this last day of September there was a crisp coolness to the air that portended the coming of winter. Neither spoke now. The servant carried a low wickerwork table which he placed between the men and then went back to the house. He reappeared, carrying this time a chipped porcelain jug, which he placed on the table, with two cups. The younger man poured out into the cups a lightly sweetened tea, flavoured with cloves, mint and cinnamon. As Steinhardt took small sips from it, he found it a bracing infusion and as its warmth spread into him, he stretched out his long legs indolently and looked expectantly at his host.

CHAPTER 2

TULSI

You first heard of Tulsi at Chandigarh, then?" the latter asked.

The younger man pursed his lips in thought for a few moments. "No", he said finally. "I'd been reading about this region and its people when I came across a passing reference to him. He was talked about as a 'holy man', which may mean anything in this country. Elsewhere, another fleeting reference described him as a fabulist—a storyteller who used fables to illustrate moral truths. That intrigued me. I know of course that there's a tradition here of presenting epics on stage at certain times of the year. I think the *Ramayan* will soon be performed over a two week period".

Steinhardt paused to take a sip of from his cup and looked at his host. The latter nodded wordlessly. "There was a similar tradition in Europe too, during the Middle Ages. 'Morality Plays', as they were called, used to be presented, in which specific virtues and vices would be personified as characters". He put his cup on the table and paused to recollect his thoughts. "Recently there has been a movement to revive this tradition and the church has put in a lot of effort into this. In fact, I've seen a beautiful presentation of John Bunyan's ` The Pilgrim's Progress', by an itinerant preacher. Bunyan was probably the greatest moralist in all of English literature, and the story one of the great allegories. But that presentation was different in one very significant sense". Prasad was looking intently at his guest as he stopped speaking.

"I haven't heard of anybody who uses stories that he apparently makes up himself. And from all accounts, Tulsi does just that. Shortly after I'd read about him, I came to these parts to do some mountaineering. And while I was here, I met somebody who had been to one of his story telling sessions. It was then that I learned about some of the peculiar features of his . . . stories". There was the barest of pauses before Steinhardt pronounced the last word.

The older man nodded encouragingly. "Yes", he said thoughtfully. "It did occur to me that it was something like that which had brought you here. You see, quite a few foreigners like you come here out of curiosity. And I think most of them go away disappointed. It's difficult to separate the fact from all those stories that have gathered around him". Prasad stopped to look at his guest before continuing. "In fact, I don't see how you could go about verifying anything. The people here are mostly tribals, willing to believe things which would appear fantastic to anybody who doesn't belong to these parts. Speaking for myself, I've seen some odd things here. Come to think of it . . ." Prasad stopped, leaned back in his chair, closed his eyes and apparently sank into a reverie. The other man waited patiently for his host to come out of it.

"Anyway, tell me. You came here to meet him. What happened then?" Prasad asked finally.

Steinhardt shook his head. "Nothing. I couldn't meet him. He wanders around so much that it's pretty difficult to trace his whereabouts".

"The wind bloweth where it listeth?" asked his host.

"Exactly", acknowledged the mathematician with a grin. "But I didn't give up easily. I did try one or two places around here that he'd reportedly been seen in. It was then that I came to learn about his habit of holding his sessions only on full moon nights. Is that correct?"

"That's right. In fact, it's not even on all full moon nights. I would say, maybe three or four times a year". A cool breeze had sprung up by this time and shreds of cloud floated across the full, bright disc of the moon. "So, when you heard that he was going to talk at Macholi, you saw your chance?"

It was a full minute before Steinhardt spoke. "That is true. But there was something else also", he said finally. He stood up now. "I'd like to show you something", he said. He started walking towards the house and in a dozen long strides had reached the verandah. He took the three steps in one effortless bound, opened the door and disappeared inside. Five minutes later, he was back at the table. Prasad saw that he had brought his bag. Opening this, the standing man withdrew from it a black plastic box about a meter in length and as his host watched wonderingly, he touched what must have been a switch at its side. A pearly panel on the side facing Prasad lit up now. "It's a combination of a light and a tape recorder, operated by a battery", explained the mathematician. He now looked through the contents of the valise and extracted a folder. Riffling swiftly through the papers in it, he finally withdrew one carefully and handed it to the sitting man. "I think there's enough light for you to read it comfortably, if you stretch forward a bit", he said.

CHAPTER 3

THE MACHOLI DIGS

Prasad took the sheet of paper and glanced curiously at it. It was a photocopy of what he took to be the first page of a journal article, carrying an abstract and an eighty five year old dateline.

ABSTRACT

Excavations near Macholi in Lahaul-Spiti region of North Western India have uncovered a small thousand year old township. Several metal artifacts like brass and copper coins and knives have been found. But the most remarkable feature that has come to light pertains to several stone and brick structures within a roughly square enclosure fifteen meters to the side. Most of these structures were intended to house metal discs and tubes, some of which were unearthed at the site. The former were between half to one metre in diameter.

Some of the discs are of metal, with holes about a centimetre to five centimetres in diameter drilled exactly through their centers. There are sufficient clues to indicate that the discs were mounted on platforms by rods fixed into the platforms in the plane of the discs. There was a lot of speculation about the purpose these structures served. Several theories were put forward, which covered a gamut of possibilities from a site for religious rites—even a sacrificial altar—to a more secular function, like a venue for state ceremonials. When the riddle was finally cracked, it astonished the academic circles. The whole ensemble has been identified as a small, but—by the standards of its time—an extremely sophisticated observatory. The discs, properly aligned, could perhaps be used to locate the positions of various celestial bodies.

The find raises some fascinating questions:

(i) Given that there is no reason to believe that astronomical knowledge *in any part of the world* around the time the observatory had been built had reached a level of expertise that could even begin to be compared with that of the Macholi structures, where did such expertise come from?

(ii) On the other hand, if it is to be argued that the people in that region had reached corresponding levels of advancement in other departments of cultural and technological fields, as would surely become necessary, it is a matter of some puzzlement that they have left so little tangible evidence for it, other than the observatory.

After he had finished its perusal, Prasad carefully lifted one end of the recorder, placed the paper under it and leaned back in this chair. For a while neither man spoke. Steinhardt leaned forward and switched off the light. "That's interesting. I've never heard anything about this excavation thing", said Prasad.

The visitor nodded slowly. "It's a bit surprising to me that it didn't attract greater attention, at that time or afterwards, considering that we don't have a ghost of an explanation for what's been found. But I suppose there were reasons for that. One I can think of is that the war intervened before the work could be continued and after that it just fell out of sight of the academic mainstream, for no particular reason".

Steinhardt stopped as his host refilled his cup from the jug. He kept staring broodingly at the cup for a full minute. "But then, I suppose, academic preoccupations are as much subject to the ebb and flow of fashion as the length of this year's skirt's hemline", he continued. He looked at the older man. "Do you know that the ruins of Troy were discovered by an inspired amateur? Archaeology is no longer an individual's province, of course. Knowledge has inevitably fragmented into areas of specialty, and has all but killed off the tribe of gifted amateurs". The mathematician raised the cup to his lips and delicately took a sip from it.

"But one is always tempted?" asked Prasad with a smile.

"One is always tempted", the mathematician echoed, with an answering smile.

"Which means, I gather, that you have a theory about this business?" It was more a statement than a question from the older man.

Steinhardt smiled. "No sir. I implied no such thing. In fact, if I did have an inkling, I wouldn't be here now".

"Ah, yes", said the other. "I was waiting for you to come to that".

"Oh, I'll tell you about that. But you're probably going to be disappointed by the reason. But before that I want a favour from you. I want to hear everything you know about . . . . what's his name? . . . . Tusli . . . . No . . . . Tulsi . . . .".

"Tulsi Ata" said the other helpfully.

"Right", said Steinhardt briskly. There was a self conscious little smile now as he looked at his host. "I've reached the point when I'm not quite sure what has really brought me here—whether it's curiosity about Tulsi or the Macholi digs".

CHAPTER 4

THE ITINERANT AESOP

"So, with your permission now, I'm going to do something which I hope you won't think odd. You see, I thought it best to record your account on tape", said Steinhardt. As his host watched, he got up, inserted a cassette into the recorder, snapped the chamber shut and looked at Prasad expectantly.

"All this is making me rather nervous", said Prasad with a smile.

"No need to ", replied the other quickly, "I assure you nobody will listen to it except me. And it saves me the trouble of making notes. Shall we begin, then?"

Prasad looked thoughtfully at the recorder, then asked, "Could I have few minutes to compose my ideas?"

"Certainly", said the mathematician". They sat in silence for ten minutes at the end of which the older man cleared his throat and nodded. Steinhardt switched on the player now.

"I'll begin with the name. I think the man's strangeness begins with his name itself". Prasad was speaking slowly, in an effort to make his enunciation as clear as possible. "In the language spoken here, the word `Ata' means a bridge. But to make matters more confusing, there's a river by that name not far from here. So the word may refer possibly to a bridge over that river, or to the river itself. The man commonly goes by the name of Tulsi here, except on certain special occasions. What these are I shall explain in a minute. As for Tulsi, it's difficult—almost impossible—to get him to talk about himself, or part with any personal details. If one asks him where he comes from, for instance, he responds with the vague term 'Yonder' and waves his hand over half the points of the compass. Either he can't or won't say. In any case, he's reclusive and rarely speaks.

There are two aspects to his personality. These two aspects are so different that one can almost say he's two persons fused into one. In the first of these, he wanders around these parts apparently making a living by doing odd jobs. He may repair a fence here, chop some wood there, do some gardening work—whatever comes his way. I think it can be said that he doesn't display any expert knowledge or skill of any sort at any of these activities. On one occasion, I understand that he worked at a small wayside hostelry—called *dhabas* in this part of the country—for a couple of months, washing dishes. This is rather exceptional for him, since he rarely stays longer than a few days at any place. It's not an uncommon experience here for somebody to hire him one morning and find him gone the next morning without bothering to collect his wage. This unworldliness, if you may call it such, has earned him the reputation of a holy man. Which is odd—for some of his habits hardly conform to the ascetic code under which *sadhus*—as holy men are known in this country—live. For instance, he is reliably known to eat meat. I have heard also that he's not above drinking liquor or smoking. My enquiries have revealed also that in all his wanderings he does not carry any personal effects beyond one or two changes of clothing, perhaps. In fact, on more than one occasion, he's been known to give away his clothes and even his money, to anybody whom he felt needed it more than he did. Once, in Shimla, I met a person who assured me he'd seen Tulsi begging in the marketplace there. But this is not a fact I could find anybody to attest to.

He's not known to go very far from this place, though he periodically disappears, when no one sees him for months. Where he goes or what he does during these absences is a mystery. In fact, to my knowledge, nobody has seen him outside this region. This is one reason why I'm inclined to put down the account of his begging in a Shimla market to a case of mistaken identity, though it has to be admitted that there is nothing about his known character or personality that would make one dismiss the story out of hand. He speaks a queer mixture of the vernacular and a dialectical variant of it spoken in the tribal areas. There is nothing else which sets him apart from any other person of his class in this part of the country. All this enables him to live under conditions of an anonymity that I'm sure he doesn't find unwelcome".

The narration ceased. Prasad stopped now and signalled to the other man to switch off the machine. "Just give me a few minutes", he said. Steinhardt nodded.

The older man leaned back, clasped his hands loosely in this lap and gazed absently at the valley sweeping down before him. The moonlit loveliness of the scene must have entranced the guest. He got up, walked a few paces to the edge of the lawn and stood looking down at it. Presently, hearing his name called, he turned around and walked back. "You can start the recording now", said Prasad. When Steinhardt had switched on the recorder, Prasad took up the narration again.

"I come now to the second and remarkable aspect of his personality. It's not reliably known when he was first seen here. There are enough nondescript individuals of his type wandering around here for him not to attract any attention. Sadly, most of these are drug addicts who work as itinerant labour. But I think it was about fifteen years ago that he preached his first sermon—if I may call it that. It was a full moon day. Not far from this place, there is a large, shallow, saucer-shaped depression in the land, called Kandheri. Exactly in the center of it there's a small shrine housing a local deity. Every year on the full moon day in May, there's a festival at Kandheri. The people of the area throng there and the night is spent in the kind of merrymaking that is typical of such festivals.

On this night, there was the usual group of men sitting outside the little temple, partaking of the special sweetmeats that are cooked in a community kitchen behind the shrine. Now, I'm not quite sure of the details of what I'm going to narrate and at places I have been obliged to fill with surmise the gaps in the version I was told. With this caveat, I shall continue.

The talk among the men had turned to the festival and when it had started being an annual custom. The general belief here is that the tradition started as a harvest festival with the building of the temple seventy or eighty years ago. The strongest evidence in favour of this hypothesis is the fact that the traditional ceremonial repast includes a dish from an oat-like cereal that had been extensively grown in that part then. One of those present declared that as a child he had been told by his grandfather, who had worked with British surveyors, that according to the records compiled by them, the temple had been built two hundred years ago and the festival had started then, to commemorate the consecration.

Tulsi, who was present, now spoke. He matter-of-factly announced that the festival that was taking place on that day was the two thousand two hundred and seventy third occasion of its celebration. When the flabbergasted group looked at him, suspecting a joke of some sort, he stuck to his claim. In fact, he went on to say that in all those years, on seventy times the festival had been missed owing to wars, pestilences or other catastrophes. None in that assembly must have doubted that they were in the presence of a madman. When somebody sarcastically suggested that he might as well fill in a couple of other details like how, why and by whom the tradition had been begun, Tulsi promptly took him at his word. He got up, went into the shrine and came out with a little earthen lamp which he placed in a small niche on the wall. He seated himself on the floor of the temple and started his story.

By this time, the congregation had grown to around twenty to thirty people. And as Tulsi started speaking, word spread and a large and curious throng had collected". Prasad paused now, poured out some tea into his cup and took a sip from it before continuing.

"I was fortunate enough to meet somebody who was of the assembly who had heard Tulsi for the first time. I am, therefore, reasonably confident that this account is substantially true and where there is any discrepancy with fact, the inaccuracy would not be very significant. The story that Tulsi related was broadly this. Around three thousand years ago, there had been a huge river flowing through the region. In its course, it had flowed into the Kandheri cavity at one end and out through the other, forming a natural lake. During many centuries that followed, the river had dried up and finally, and after some years, so had the lake. The people had then prayed to their deity to restore their water and had promised a figurine to honour her if their entreaty were to be granted. Shortly after this, from a point in the centre of the dried up lake, a fountain of water had spurted up, filling up the lake. The grateful people had kept their promise and installed a stone statue of their deity, in the water. Presently, after many more centuries the water had again dried up. This time the people living there had migrated, looking for a place where the water would be more plentiful. Much later, when the knowledge of the lake and its water had faded out of living memory, the people living in the region had built a small shrine around the statuary. Meanwhile, through all these vicissitudes, the tradition of the annual festival had been kept alive". The narrator paused for a brief moment.

"It has to be acknowledged that there is nothing implausible about the theory, if such it was", he continued.

"From a hydrological point of view, it is not uncommon to find artesian wells in regions which have had plenty of water at one time. And the geographical peculiarity of the saucer shaped cavity makes it even more likely. And there were several implications of the theory which made some features of it readily verifiable. For example, it would not be a difficult thing to test the age of the statuary. Or for that matter, the stones used in building the walls of the shrine. But when I first heard of the story, I must confess that, like everybody else, I could not take it seriously enough to think of testing it out. And it would not have been an easy matter, even if I'd been so minded. As for Tulsi's audience, it can be safely assumed that the thought of subjecting the story to a test would not have crossed anybody's mind. They were a lot of simple villagers who loved a good story and were prepared to leave it at that, without going into the question of examining its congruity with fact.

This was, of course, the first of many such performances. For some reason known only to himself, these occasions have always been on a full moon day. And the lighted lamp also became a constant feature of his discourses. In fact, he now uses this method to announce his storytelling. The day before the full moon, there would be a lighted lamp placed at a clearly visible place in a temple. The people of the region would know immediately that they were being invited for a story. The size of the congregation these days would be anything up to two hundred. They are growing in popularity. And there has been one significant change from his original talk, with regard to the themes that Tulsi discourses on. There is a clearly discernible moral element on which they are based. In that sense they are more parables than mere stories. But it must be emphasised that the moral principle is always allowed to remain implicit—for, the fabulist never departs from his story line to offer moral or ethical reflections. I have listened to quite a few of his sermons and have always found them to be consistent with this observation. Further, in my opinion, these stories, or parables, or whatever you may want to call them, are of striking originality. They involve complex, strongly drawn characters who respond in unusual ways in a crisis. There was a scholar from the University of Berlin who had come to hear him once. He told me that some of Tulsi's stories are reminiscent of the themes used by the great playwright Bertolt Brecht. I suggest to anybody who is interested, the problem of explaining how a person without the rudiments of anything that could be called education—in fact, there is ample reason to believe that Tulsi is illiterate—can come up with these creations. It is a task that is entirely beyond my powers.

I have a feeling that if Tulsi himself were asked about this and if he were minded to answer, he would reply that he *never reported anything that did not happen*. For, it is an oddity of his that he always speaks as if he saw (or in some cases, would see) the events that he speaks about. One even gets an odd feeling sometimes that he had a personal acquaintance with the remarkable characters around whom he creates his stories. I met him only once. On that occasion, I finally managed to get him to talk about himself. He told me then that he is "sometimes able to see the Earth when she is dreaming". Nor would he say anything more. Maybe he means he is possessed by visions which come to him spontaneously. It's also possible that these are inspired by certain narcotics".

Nor is this the only queer feature of his performance. There was one other which did not escape the informant who had spoken to me about the first time Tulsi had spoken in public. This was, in fact, something that has become more and more evident in his subsequent talks. He said that when Tulsi starts on the narration of one of his stories, a subtle change would come over him. It's something that's difficult to describe and which I myself have noticed upon all occasions when I have been able to attend his sessions. A certain air of authority seems to descend on him. In fact, this is so obvious that when it becomes necessary for any member of the audience to speak with him, they do so with a natural respect which almost amounts to reverence. Thus, for example, they address him as "Huzoor" or "Ji" which are the conventional honorifics in this part of the country. And it does not appear particularly strange to these people that a man whom they had been used to addressing in such familiar terms a few minutes ago, should now be accorded this respect. Nor is it to be imagined that this elevation of status remains after the story has ended. After he finishes, Tulsi just gets down, mingles with the crowd and walks away. It is his custom—if the word can be properly used of someone so utterly unpredictable—that he rarely returns to the place where he has spoken once". There was a pause now while Prasad seemed to be absorbed in his thoughts.

"I must confess that nothing in all my experience has prepared me for understanding a phenomenon like this man", he concluded and signalled Steinhardt to stop the recording.

CHAPTER 5

THE MAN WHO SAW TOMORROW

The two men sat now in a silence that neither seemed to want to break. The mathematician finally stirred in his seat and looked directly at his host. "I must thank you for that", he said. "I couldn't have wished for a more complete picture. But there's just one question". The older man looked at him questioningly. "Did you at any time try to check on any of his stories? I mean, try to find out whether there was any element of fact in any of them?"

Prasad did not answer. He sat staring frowningly ahead of him for a full minute. "That's a difficult one to answer", he said finally. A small sigh escaped him. "You see, I'll be honest with you. I don't know whether to talk about these things". He lapsed into silence again and finally seemed to come to some sort of decision. "Tulsi is a very private sort of person—you might say a very shy person. You will understand that people of his sort are alarmed and confused by any kind of publicity. You know, I've seen wild animals—even a leopard, once—caught in the headlights of a car. They just stand rooted to the spot, staring at the lights, unable to move. Just paralysed, I tell you. And they are sometimes shot as they stand like that".

"I know exactly what you mean", said Steinhardt.

The other nodded slowly. "Now, if I tell you something in confidence and if it should get out, there'll be a lot of unwelcome publicity. Reporters, press conferences, the media people on the lookout for a sensational story . . . .".

"If you have any reservations on that score, I won't try to persuade you", said Steinhardt.

Prasad looked steadily into the face of the younger man. "I think I can trust you", he said slowly. "Alright. I'll tell you something that happened after I had heard the account about the first story of Tulsi's. It was some years ago and I had gone to Kandheri to look for certain flowers—If I remember right, a variety of celandines you don't find in this region—that I'd been told was growing in those parts. When I reached the Kandheri cavity, I found a crew of workmen there, digging the soil at some places and examining it at others. It turned out that they were from the geological society of India. At that time there was a huge and active project to map the course of a mighty river, Saraswathi, to which there had been intriguing references in the most ancient mythologies of India. Informed academic opinion was divided between those who believed that such a river had existed sometime and those who rejected the evidence as being too inconclusive to justify the project. Well, this expedition had come with the hope of tracing one of the river's tributaries. They were subpoenaing heaven and Earth as witness, one of the scientists in charge of the expedition jokingly told me. He explained that they were collecting data from two sources—satellite imagery from the sky and soil samples on the ground. He then asked me whether I had ever heard of a large lake or pond or a body of water filling the cavity we stood in. I said that as far as anybody knew, there had been no water there. He said that a certain kind of sandy soil and the smoothness of some pebbles there definitely hinted initially at the possibility". Prasad paused, his brow furrowing in frowning effort as he recalled the incident. "Then there was the alluvium, which, I gather, is a deposit left by water—a flood, a lake or a river that may have fed it. That was certainly a very clear indication. But, when they had dug to a deeper level, they came across shale, a kind of rock, which, I understand, is again associated with the presence of water". Prasad stopped to call out to the servant. When the latter came, he asked the tea things to be cleared from the table.

The host waited while the servant was gathering the cups and jugs and when the latter had left, took up the narration again. "I didn't give the incident much thought", he said. "But one day the curious coincidence struck me. Almost on a whim, I wrote to my brother in the university geology department. Could he write to the expedition leader who had come here and ask him whether they had been able to reach any conclusions about the rock samples they had gathered at Kandheri? I must tell you that in the intervening period there had been a change of government and with it a change of policy. In the altered political environment, the new government had found it expedient to abandon the Saraswathi project. But the expedition's leader did not find it difficult to look into the records and find the information I'd asked for. The report that he sent me contained some formidable technical jargon. First, there was some clayey soil—agillaceous or something they called it. And then . . . . What was it now . . . Stromabolites . . . . Stromatolites . . . . or something". Prasad pushed back his chair and got to his feet. "I'll get you the report. You may find it interesting". Steinhardt quickly motioned him back into the chair. "It's hardly worth the bother", he said firmly. "I haven't any idea about these things. Besides, your account is getting far too interesting. Let's forget the report and its technical details for now". Prasad seated himself again. "Anyway, to summarise the contents of the report, on the basis of tests and observations made on the samples, there had undeniably been a large lake at Kandheri, about three thousand years ago". Prasad stopped to look at the other man. "Tell me what you would have done in my position, professor Stei . . . Bruce?"

Steinhardt massaged his chin for a moment before he spoke. "Kept it to myself, certainly", he said.

CHAPTER 6

THE MYSTERY

Another silence descended now. "Now I've answered your question, will you answer one of mine?"

Steinhardt grinned. "Sure", he said. "Are you going to ask me whether there was any reason besides wanting to hear Tulsi that brought me here?"

"Exactly", answered his host. Steinhardt's fingers drummed a rapid tattoo on the table top. "I told you I'd been to Macholi earlier, on a mountaineering expedition. I'd been staying with a family in a house here. They had a room to spare and it suited me perfectly. In fact, the man who gave it to me was a man I'd hired as a porter during my climb earlier. I have a gift for picking up languages and I came to know him pretty well and it was from him that I first came to know about Tulsi. He also told me that Tulsi went by a name that meant 'The man who saw tomorrow', or something like that". Steinhardt tapped his brow with his forefinger. "I used to remember the term".

"*Kal ko dekne wale?*" suggested the other. "Right", said Steinhardt gratefully. "That's it. Isn't there a pun on that first word? I think it means 'yesterday' as well as 'tomorrow'".

The other man nodded with a smile. "The pun is unintended; but exquisitely appropriate. I listened to a story of his once. He began it by remarking quite casually that at a time in the future when the events of what he was going to narrate would take place, the valley we were sitting in would be flooded by a large lake. When somebody in the audience asked how that can happen without a river, his answer was that the water would form from a lot of ice melting".

"Oh, oh", said Steinhardt. "Our friend seems pretty well informed about global warming and the melting of glaciers".

"Seems like that, wouldn't it? But I've taken you away from your story".

"There really isn't very much more", replied Steinhardt. "I got curious and pressed him for details. He said Tulsi could see hundreds of years into the past. He accepted that bit unquestioningly. Understandable, of course. I wouldn't have expected too much skepticism, anyway". He paused. "For that matter, I don't think I'm much of a sceptic myself", he grinned. "Take this Macholi observatory business, for instance. It was a niggling presence in my mind. I'd come across a reference to that journal article when I was reading about something else; but I took it seriously enough to see what I could find out about it. In fact, I went to Cambridge looking for the author of that article". Steinhardt stopped and shook his head slowly. "But it was a dead end there. I discovered that the person who had been in charge of the team that had done the excavation work had been killed in the war. And after the war, nobody had thought of continuing the work. Even worse, the records of the work done at Macholi were either lost or misplaced and there was not a chance that after all these years, especially with a war helpfully happening at the right time, anything could be found out about it. As for the discs and tubes themselves, they had been sent for cleaning. The institute which had been entrusted with the work had been temporarily requisitioned for military purposes and as far as I could discover, the rooms where the discs had been lying had been used as transit stations for troops which had been billeted there. After the war ended, nobody had a clue to where they had gone. I gave up at that point".

He paused before continuing. "But, at Cambridge, I did manage to learn some curious facts. The archaeologist who had been leading the Macholi expedition was professor Norman Cowley. By one of those odd coincidences that give a decisive turn to events, it turned out that Cowley's widow was known well to a cousin of mine. To make a long story short, I cadged an invitation to visit her. When she learned about my interest, she allowed me to see her husband's papers among which I found a mass of notes on the work that had been carried out at Macholi, with several photographs and diagrams. Cowley could possibly have been preparing them for publication when the war intervened. Anyway, I got photocopies made of whatever I thought looked interesting. Then I started poring over them in earnest". Steinhardt stopped to look at his host and found the latter watching him intently.

"Nothing made sense", confessed the mathematician with a shake of his head. "For one thing, I was looking at a two dimensional representation of *spatial* configurations. So that, when I started making cardboard models, I began to understand certain things. Some of the discs, for example, had been permanently fixed in place, by being fused into certain positions on straight rods, which would allow them to be manoeuvred into any desired position. It was obvious that their alignments suggested that they had been used to observe some positions in the sky—a fact that I would not have expected Cowley to notice. *But why?* Intrigued, I decided to inform myself about astronomy. I enrolled myself for an elementary university course, read up books and even bought a simple telescope".

Prasad's eyes widened. "You are a methodical man", he said.

The other nodded. "Well, I've been called that. Anyway, the more astronomy I learned, the more what I'd started calling in my mind 'The mystery of the Macholi digs', began to grow on me. A big reason for this was a fundamental discovery I made after I began my studies. You see, I've told you that the care that had been taken to fix those discs in certain positions didn't make any sense to me—I mean somebody had obviously taken very great pains *in adjusting them very precisely in certain directions* and though the apparatus was rudimentary by our standards, it was clear that it must have allowed a precision that must have been simply stunning for its time. The puzzle was, why? What was so terribly interesting about those positions? There was nothing in that quarter of the sky that was even remotely interesting. I must confess that when the solution finally came to me, I felt pretty silly. The simple fact was that the people who had made those fantastically precise adjustments had been looking at *entirely different celestial configurations.* The skies of their own time, in other words".

Steinhardt stopped to shift his position in his chair. He lifted up a knee and hooked his clasped hands over it. "Well?", prompted the older man now.

"With the kind of information resources available these days, it took me about a week to figure out what the builders of that observatory had been gazing at". Steinhardt paused again, pursed his lips with a frown and gazed absently at infinity, while Prasad waited patiently. "There were enough indicators to suggest that they must have been surveying *all the planets* and had, in fact, logged some of their observations as pictorial representations of the configurations on brass discs. What must have made the deciphering an impossibly difficult task for Cowley, of course, was that the discs had been pitted and scored by long interment, so that it required hours of careful examination to distinguish the genuine markings. And as for me, you have to remember I was working not with the discs themselves but with their photographs, which were rarely of good enough quality. So, everything said and done, in all fairness I'll have to grant that there is a provisionality about some of my conclusions. More so since I'm far from being an expert in this area". Steinhardt broke off his narration to direct a glance at his host. "Do you know any astronomy?" he asked.

The other shook his head diffidently by way of answer. "Not much beyond naming the nine planets", he said.

"Alright then. I'll briefly recall a few facts. Of the eight planets visible from the Earth today, five were identified from ancient times. In some instances, millennia before the Christian era. But the three smaller planets—Neptune, Uranus and Pluto—were not sighted till much later. Neptune, for instance, was discovered through the techniques of mathematical perturbation theory around 1850. It is likely that Galileo saw it using the telescope he had constructed, around 1610. But he possibly mistook it for a star. Uranus was sighted by Flamsteed in 1690, while Pluto was discovered in 1930". The mathematician paused. "You see what I'm driving at?"

Prasad nodded slowly. "How did these people come by this knowledge hundreds of years ago?"

"Precisely. And that's not all. When you remember that these *three planets can be seen only through a telescope,* the plot thickens. The only reasonable assumption is that these people, whoever they were, had some working version of a telescope. That would imply, in turn, that they had *lenses* and a knowledge of telescope casings. And much more importantly, *telescope mountings".* Steinhardt stopped speaking to shake his head in wonderment.

"Galileo is credited with constructing the first telescope at the beginning of the seventeenth century", he continued. "A few years before that, Dutch spectacle makers seemed to have hit upon the general principle of aligning lenses to enhance their magnifying effect".

"But if they had employed lenses, wouldn't they have left some evidence of it?" Prasad interrupted.

"If they did, there was certainly no evidence of it. Remember that Cowley was not an astronomer and would not necessarily have recognized any evidence he would come across. But an even more intriguing possibility suggests itself to me", continued Steinhardt. "To extend this fairy tale one more step, could they have used lenses unlike the traditional glass ones? For example, liquid lenses? Whatever the answer is, I'll tell you now about the most perplexing part of the whole matter. There's reason to believe that *bamboo tubes were used in combination with metal ones* in some parts of the fixture. You see, when you come across missing sections of tubing, you have to assume that somebody must have used tubes of *biodegradable* material which would crumble to dust over a thousand year interment". Steinhardt stopped to see the effect the disclosure had on the older man.

"So it would appear that two groups of people were responsible for constructing the instruments. Could it be that one of them came earlier. Possibly the later group had come upon the instruments left by the earlier".

Steinhardt shrugged. "It's possible, of course. Or, for some reason we can have no inkling of, the same group of persons had used extremely sophisticated as well fairly primitive apparatuses at the same time. But all this still does not explain how those instruments came to be there at that time, when telescopes and the even more formidable problem of their mountings were hundreds of years into the future".

Steinhardt paused to comb his beard with his long fingers. "A few years after that material came into my hands, I came out here to look at Macholi for myself.

What I found here was even more frustrating. Nobody seemed to know anything about the archaelogical site and I couldn't even find out where the place was . . .ʺ

ʺThere isn't much chance of your finding it after all this time", interrupted Prasad. "This area is prone to landslides big and small, and something with the dimensions described by you can quite easily get covered up".

ʺThat's one mystery less, then", said the mathematician thoughtfully. "Anyway, my pre-occupation with this matter would quite often get snowed under by a lot of more pressing concerns most of the time. And then, for no reason or other, it would suddenly emerge. I think it would have gone on like that if I hadn't been told, quite accidentally, that Tulsi was going to tell one of his stories at Macholi. And I've heard that the locales for the tales he comes up with are always places very close to where he's holding his soiree". Steinhardt stopped now to look at his host. "A fantastic notion flashed into my mind", he said slowly. "What if he should say something that throws some light on the Macholi digs?" He paused before continuing. "I'd no idea of this story of yours at that time, of course. But I must confess that the fact I can entertain the possibility shocks me in my saner moments".

ʺI can understand that", said the other with a smile. "It's not something that you would like to have advertised".

ʺExactly", replied Steinhardt. "But even then it was an impulse that brought me here. But after listening to your Kandheri story . . . .".

Steinhardt leaned back and stretched his tall frame languorously. Prasad was silent for a minute or two. "Let's hope that you will be repaid for your pains", he said finally, with an expression that the other could not quite read. He then consulted his watch. "I think I'll go in and lie down for an hour or two. We have time enough for that. I usually go to bed around ten. But today . . . ."

"Look. If this junket is going to mean that kind of dislocation in your schedule, I would have absolutely no difficulty in going alone".

"No, no. That's not what I meant at all. For that matter, I've been looking forward to it myself ever since my servant brought home the news about today's performance". He got up now. "If you'll excuse me . . . .". The other nodded.

CHAPTER 7

THE CURTAIN GOES UP

For sometime after his host's departure, the mathematician sat wrapped up in his own thoughts. He then slowly leaned forward, switched on the player and started listening to his host's recital. Every now and then he would stop the player, switch on the light and make some notings in a diary he had taken from his bag. Presently he switched off the player and sat contemplating the scene before him. He then fell into a light doze. He had no notion of how long he had been sitting there when he was awakened by the light touch of the older man's arm on his shoulder. "It's almost time", said Prasad.

"Give me a minute", said his guest and carrying the player, disappeared into the house. He emerged a few minutes later and Prasad saw that he had removed his travel stained clothes and got into a fresh shirt. There was a light looking leather case which was slung on Steinhardt's shoulder by a long strap. Prasad guessed that it contained the player.

He got up now, called to the servant to carry the table and chairs inside and then started walking towards the car. But instead of getting into it, he went around it and came away wheeling a motor bicycle. "I thought first we'd go by car", he said, "then changed my mind and decided that the bike would be more comfortable for you".

"That's fine", said the other, "But if you don't mind, I think it's best if you get on behind me, since I'm bigger and much heavier than you. I'd be able to handle the machine better. I don't think there's much chance I'd lose my way".

The suggestion was followed. The bike now roared along the road, shattering the stillness of the night. Though there was no traffic on the road, they however passed a few groups of people talking softly among themselves and in a few minutes had reached the foot of the low hill, at a point where a flight of steps ascended to the temple at the top. It was not a difficult ascent for the two men, though at a few points on the way, their progress had to be interrupted to allow Prasad to regain his wind. The tall figure of the mathematician attracted some attention from some of those walking up among whom there was an unmistakable air of merriment as at a fair or a festival. Steinhardt noted that quite a few people seemed to know the older man and exchanged greetings with him. During one of the breaks he asked the question that had been uppermost in his mind now. "Does he allow himself to be photographed?", he asked.

The other man looked at him quickly. There was a concern in his voice that was unmistakable as he spoke: "Tulsi, you mean? Why do you ask? Have you brought a camera or one of those video things?"

"Not at all", said the other with a chuckle. "I did think of something like that, but abandoned the idea when you told me about the kind of effect it may have on him".

"It's a good decision", said Prasad, with evident relief.

A worried frown appeared on the face of the younger man now. "Will a voice recording be OK?", he asked.

The other patted him reassuringly. "He's never objected to it till now. Don't worry. If there's any problem, I'll handle it".

When they had climbed the last step, they found themselves in a spacious courtyard in front of the temple. Steinhardt estimated there should have been about a hundred and fifty people assembled there. The crowd was sitting on the ground; some on thick blankets which had been spread out over the earth. Some were smoking and the rank smell of uncured tobacco assailed the nostril. Others were talking in hushed tones and there was a general air of expectancy hanging over the assembly. Prasad made his way to the front. There was a small raised platform, about a meter wide and two meters in length on either side of the entrance to the temple. Above the platform on the right, in a small niche in the wall, a little earthen lamp was burning, its flame unmovingly steady, so that it looked as if it had been painted there. Prasad seated himself on the ground and motioned his companion to do so beside him. Steinhardt joined him and busied himself with getting his tape recorder ready. As he was checking his instruments, two men who were obviously priests, came out of the temple. One of them went around distributing a large leaf of some plant, while the other scooped out a dish from a battered bucket that he carried, and with a quick and practiced gesture, placed a dollop of it on the leaf held in readiness for it. The mathematician who knew enough of the local custom, quickly removed his shoes and with a little curtesy of thanks, received his share. After a few minutes the priests went in, their task finished. The conversation started again.

Steinhardt, who had been bent over his recorder, absorbed in its settings, suddenly realized that the talk had died out and looked up quickly. He was just in time to see the figure of a man emerge from the shadow at the side of the temple. It was a slightly built figure, not over five and a half feet in height, Steinhardt decided. Tulsi, for it must have been certainly he, was walking slowly. As he came around the platform and took his seat there, there was a general shuffling of feet and everybody stood up. Tulsi now settled himself comfortably, cross legged as was the custom; then faced the assembly before him, raised his hands and joined them together before him, in the timeless and universal Hindu gesture of salutation. He did it now with the languorous sweep of his arms that had the grace of a butterfly's wings coming together. Everybody now sat down slowly. The mathematician looked at him with curiosity. It was difficult to assess his age. He could have been anywhere from thirty to sixty; but remembering all he had heard, Steinhardt decided it would be nearer the latter figure. From where he sat, in the dark, deep shadow of the platform, it was impossible to make out anything of his features, except the coal black beard that fell to his chest. A kind of long shirt of what appeared to be some coarse cotton material covered the upper part of his body, with the buttons open at the chest and the sleeves reaching half way between his wrist and elbow, while a shawl or a blanket was wrapped about his shoulders. He seemed to be sunk in a trance now, his eyes closed. Presently Tulsi opened his eyes and swept the gathering before him with a glance. He was sitting with his back ramrod straight, his hands resting lightly in his lap.

He began speaking slowly, intoning every syllable with a deliberate clearness—so that Steinhardt, to his relief, found it fairly easy to follow what was said. Tulsi's eyes were fixed on a man sitting a few feet behind where the two men sat. "Sukh Ram", said the speaker, with a disconcerting directness, "how much land have you?" A titter ran round the crowd. Prasad now leaned over to his companion and whispered that the man addressed was the richest person in that region. The man thus spoken to, plainly appeared discomfited by the unexpected query. He squirmed a bit and looked around him. There was a general enjoyment of his unease and everybody near him craned forward to hear what he would say. He held a brief, whispered consultation with a man near him before rising to his feet in an attitude of respectfulness and answering. "Huzoor", he replied, "my family owns many hundred acres in these parts".

Tulsi seemed to be contemplating the answer, then nodded almost imperceptibly to himself. He was silent now. There was another whispered footnote from Prasad now to his guest. "Do you remember the transformation I spoke to you about, when Tulsi starts speaking at these sessions of his? It's very much in evidence now. Tulsi would never normally address Sukh Ram by name. There's too much difference between them in the social scale. And notice also how respectfully Sukh Ram answered him. Their roles are now spontaneously reversed". The younger man nodded thoughtfully, without taking his eyes off the figure seated before him. He was to find that this habit of sinking into silences was Tulsi's invariable custom during his narrations. It came in handy now for Prasad to keep issuing from time to time a scrics of whispered explanations about some part of the narrative that might have been obscure to the younger man otherwise. The latter began speaking again now.

"There are people in this country who own even more land. And there are people in this world who are so rich that they can buy up all the land you have", the speaker was looking again at Sukh Ram now, "and would not think much about it". The slow speech stopped now. "There are a few men who can buy all the land you can see from here. Who is the richest man in the world? Nobody knows". The narration ceased now.

CHAPTER 8

TULSI STARTS A STORY

"There once lived a man in these parts, a very, very long time ago, who was the richest man who ever lived. He was that because he owned the Earth. He lived not far from here and yet, owning the Earth as he did, he did not claim a single blade of grass as his own. When he ended his days, he lived in a monk's cell. And he died as he lived. For, when he died his body was not burnt on a sandalwood pyre. It was disposed off as any common man's might have been, by his express wish—the wood that was piled on his pyre was cut with his own hand. And none knew how rich he was, since he did not wish to talk about such things. It is true he had no title deeds to press his claim—even if he had been so minded. It was a curious situation. But it was nothing compared to the chain of events by which he came to acquire this vast dominion. That was unbelievable indeed". Tulsi lapsed into one of his silences again.

"In those days this part of the country was carved up into a number of kingdoms or principalities. Some of these were so small that Golu here could run around the boundary of it in half a day". The man referred to enjoyed something of the reputation of being a champion athlete in that region, explained Prasad, and excelled in annual rural sports events. Golu clearly enjoyed the attention he was getting.

"One of these was a little kingdom known as Vithalla", Tulsi said. There had been a king ruling over the little tract that constituted his realm.

As the narrative unfolded, a vision gradually arose of a small rural commune whose main occupation was agriculture. It was a time when men had little control over their lives and lived as long as Nature allowed them. Nature was a colossal living presence, to be thanked and worshipped with feasts and festivals when it was benign and placated with fasts and sacrifices when malign. There was a hereditary priesthood which decided which aspect was being displayed at any given time, through an interpretation of omens and auguries and—if you could afford the fee—prescribe the exact ritual by which a suitable God or deity, drawn from an extensive pantheon, could be propitiated. It was a world haunted by the spectre of pestilence, famine and such other natural catastrophes. But since none had known of a much better world, the human spirit could find things to be happy about. Such then was the kingdom over which the king had ruled. And, by the standards of the time, it was not a bad rule.

When the king had been a young man, he had married a commoner—a woman born into a low caste, in fact. It could be assumed that the priests would have extracted a very satisfactory remuneration to neutralize the divine displeasure that the misalliance would have incurred and thereby to deliver the king from the ensuing retribution. But the queen did not live long enough to enjoy either her elevation to royal status or her deliverance from celestial wrath. For, after almost two years to the day that she had been married, she gave birth to a son and died in doing it.

The king was inconsolable for an year or two. But, at the end of that period, when it was suggested to him that he should remarry, he was amenable to reason. After all, if the people did not want to see him without a consort, who was he to deny them their wish? The king could not be entirely blamed if it did not occur to him that his subjects had a few problems of their own to worry about, more pressing than the lack of a queen. This time, the king's senior counselors decided that they would be more careful about the consort to be, since they decided that the matter was too important to be left to their ruler. Further, had he not already demonstrated his propensity to enter into unsuitable union? Thus, after a lot of deliberation, it was finally decided that the daughter of the king of Ketaki, a kingdom thirty days march to the south, would be a most excellent alliance. The young princess' virtue and piety were most becoming and the dowry that she would bring from her prosperous kingdom would not be unwelcome.

Thus, in the fullness of time Vithalla had a new queen and the people two days of feasting. In all this tumult of celebration over the royal wedding, it was not surprising that the little two year old boy who was the prince of Vithalla was forgotten. Not that he minded it very much. The boy was by nature shy, even a little withdrawn. If anybody noticed this at the palace, they had put it down to the fact that he was missing a mother. As for his father, the responsibilities of running a kingdom doubtless came in the way of his devoting more time than his weekly visit to the nursery.

When the young queen entered her new abode, she decided that the two year old prince would be her prime responsibility. Her parents had taken every care in her upbringing and had instructed her as carefully in the etiquette of royal ceremonials as in the obligations of being a good human being. Accordingly, she made it a point to spend as much time as she could with the child and to win his love and trust. It was a conscientious rather than a successful attempt. Not that the boy was surly or in any other way resisted the attempts to be befriended. He was properly affectionate and respectful to the queen and as he grew up, mindful that everything should be exactly the way she wanted it. But the perceptive young queen realised that it was an affectionate rather than an intimate relationship. But where she erred was in thinking that this distance between them was due to the fact that the boy yearned for his mother with an intensity which did not permit him to accept any other in her place.

This was so entirely reasonable an assumption, of course, that she could not be blamed for making it. Especially when the truth was one which would not have normally occurred to anybody who did not have a much shrewder insight into human nature than the queen possessed. For, the boy had a sufficiency unto himself that comes rarely even to adults. He appeared perfectly satisfied to be left alone and sometimes even gave the impression that he preferred it. And so the queen, with a little sigh, after telling herself that she had done all she could (and none indeed could dispute she had), resigned herself to a state of affairs in which the love she gave was graciously received, rather than hungered for. It was a feeling that was reinforced five years later when she had a son of her own. This is not to suggest that she allowed the birth of her own child to create a distance between herself and her stepson. She very consciously guarded against such an instinct. But, with motherhood, the older child's queer self-sufficiency ceased to bother her. On his part, the boy became more absorbed in a contemplative quietness which first amused and then puzzled those who observed it. As he grew older, however, he began to display certain other, even more unusual traits of personality.

In those times, life as a member of a royal household meant little more than the privilege of being fed and clothed adequately and receiving what passed for education. There were, of course, innumerable instructions and drilling in royal protocol. And, lastly, the almost total isolation from the unwashed populace.

This distance from the people was a code that was not to be lightly breached except upon the four or five ceremonial occasions in the year, the young prince was told. He listened to this gravely, as he did to everything else. And then quietly inquired: "Why?" The directness of the query disconcerted the tutor to whom the prince's education had been entrusted. They were rough and uncouth in manners and speech, he was told. And they had dangerous diseases. Could not the royal physician treat them, the prince persisted. That was impossible, the tutor replied. There were too many of them. Then why not train more physicians, the gentle query continued, as if the prince were pursuing a personal line of enquiry to its logical conclusion.

The teacher was a venerable old greybeard who had grown wizened in teaching three generations of royalty. He had close connections with the royal household, being descended from a cadet branch a few generations ago. In his dealings with generations of royal scions, he had learned to classify his wards according to a system of private rating which assigned to each a mixture of three qualities—dullness, docility and surly arrogance—in varying proportions. His latest charge did not seem to fit the royal pattern, the tutor wryly decided. But he was not going to be cowed by a questioning princeling. Forthwith, he launched into an impromptu discourse on political economy. "Your majesty must remember that it is not as simple as you imagine. We will have to set up an institute first to train a corps of physicians. Then open hospitals where the people may come and be treated. And then provide them with medicines. Where does your majesty suggest we find the money for all this?", he asked, softening what he considered to be the brutal unanswerability of that question, with a smile. The boy looked at him for a moment, wide eyed, allowing the question to sink in.

"Why not from the taxes we collect from them? After all, it's their money, isn't it?", he then asked.

Something like respect now stirred in the old teacher's cynical breast. He contemplated his student thoughtfully. "Your majesty speaks with a wisdom which is beyond your years", he said finally. That day was to mark a turning point in the relationship between the tutor Tara Chand and his ward. Tara Chand was a man of learning and fortunately for the young prince, that learning went much farther than the functional literacy and the fundamental reckoning that the old man was expected to teach and which quite often represented an achievement that went far beyond the intellectual abilities of the princely scions who passed under his tutelage. But he found now a student of an entirely different caliber. The prince effortlessly absorbed everything that he was supposed to be taught, in a few months. He then began to question Tara Chand on the world which lay outside the palace walls and indeed about the wider world that lay beyond the contours of his realm. When young, Tara Chand had travelled extensively within his country and had gone so far as to reach the ocean that washed its shores. He had also traversed the terrain of that region many times and had come to acquire a reasonably good knowledge of it. This he communicated to the prince, as well as giving him an idea of the world of learning that lay outside.

CHAPTER 9

A FLASH IN THE NIGHT

Under the circumstances, it was perhaps natural that the young prince began to prefer the company of the old tutor rather than that of one closer to his age. Presently, he began to move with the teacher on terms, if not of equality, of at least one of a greater freedom than would normally be supposed of such a relationship. Their conversation, consequently, ranged farther than such an interaction required and the old tutor, on his part, found it a congenial obligation to first ignite and then respond to his pupil's wakening wonder, by discoursing on a lore whose variety spanned an amplitude of interests from the secular to the esoteric. It became a tacit understanding between them that nothing should be excluded from the ambit of such discussions.

However, the prince was to recollect much later one solitary occasion on which Tara Chand had clearly appeared reluctant to discuss something with him and had required a piece of genteel blackmail before he could be persuaded. They had been sitting late one night on the terrace of the tutor's house then. The prince's attention, as always, had been drawn by the night sky. It was the night of the new moon and star clusters, by their millions, wheeled against the huge velvet blackness. As the young man lowered his fascinated gaze for a moment, it came to rest on the serrated ridges of the tops of the mountains that formed one wall of the valley. He was about to raise his eyes back to the celestial spectacle, when he saw—or imagined, he was not sure—a flash of light on the crest of a hill. "Did you see that?" gasped the prince involuntarily.

"See what?" asked old Tara Chand, who had nodded off into a light doze. "I thought I saw something there . . . . like . . . . like a . . . ." But nothing that he could cull from his experience could serve to describe what he had seen. "I thought I saw something gleam there", he said finally."

"Maybe it was a shooting star", said the old man indifferently and rather to his companion's disappointment, closed his eyes with every intention of going back to his interrupted peace.

"No, no", said the prince indignantly. He pointed to the mountain top now. "It was there", he said. "It was as if somebody standing there had thrown a small bolt of lightning at us", he said.

But Tara Chand appeared to be in no mood to respond. "Could it be the Mountain Spirits?", asked the boy, breaking the silence. If he had meant to secure the tutor's attention, he could not have achieved it with better effect. The latter was wide awake now.

He directed a glance of withering scorn at his young pupil. "Who's been filling your head with all that rubbish?"

he asked. "Is it that senile old charlatan?" In some such wise did Tara Chand generally refer to the palace astrologer Amarnath.

"No he didn't tell me anything", replied the boy. "The servants at the palace talk about them sometimes". After a pause he added, "But who are they?"

There was no reply from Tara Chand for a full minute. "Why don't you ask the palace servants?" he asked presently.

But the boy shook his head. "My mother, the Queen, does not like my talking to them", he answered. Getting no response from the old man, the boy pensively remarked: "If you don't want to talk about it, maybe I'll ask uncle Amarnath".

Tara Chand opened his eyes now and nodded his head slowly in mock admiration. "You know how to get what you want out of me, don't you?" he said. He appeared to reach a decision. "Alright, then. If somebody has to talk to you about it, I prefer to do it myself rather than allow that old fool to peddle his mystical wares to you. Tell me what you want to know?"

"Everything you know", said the prince with a grin.

The tutor gave one of his rare smiles in return. "That is very simple", he said. "Nobody *knows* anything", he continued, allowing himself a slight emphasis on the word. He paused before adding: "But that doesn't prevent people from believing they know a lot, of course".

"In that case, tell me all you've heard", said the prince with persistence.

Tara Chand slowly arranged himself into a more comfortable position on the hard wooden bed on which he was reclining. "It began during the reign of your grandfather", he began ruminatively. "King Vikram Pal had ascended the throne when he was barely out of his boyhood. He had been ruling for some years when rumours or reports, or whatever you want to call it, began reaching the palace about some strange happenings in the mountains".

Nobody had lived there except shepherds, said Tara Chand. They would sometimes see a fire some distance away. But when they went there to investigate, they would find nobody. There would be signs that somebody had started a fire and tended it. Once, some townspeople who had gone to the forest to cut firewood, reported seeing a boy, or maybe a dwarf at some distance. "The fact that there was no human habitation in that part of the forest strained credibility".

The tutor broke off to yawn slowly, while the boy waited patiently for the narration to continue. "The king finally called two of his bravest soldiers and sent them to investigate. Mind you, there were no complaints from any shepherds and nobody had been hurt. Tara Chand nodded slowly to himself and added : "The king had a way of doing things". He was gazing at the distant mountaintop, seemingly lost in his memories.

CHAPTER 10

TARA CHAND'S STORY

This time the pause was longer. The tutor drew the coarse blanket he was wrapped in a bit closer to himself against the chill. The boy had not taken his eyes off him the while. "A full week passed and neither returned", the old man said finally. He looked at the boy who was watching him in rapt attention. "Your highness' grandfather was no poltroon", he continued. "At the end of the week, he chose half a dozen of his personal bodyguards and set out for the mountains. I doubt whether anybody knew the purpose of the expedition. The palace officials were told that the king was going on a hunt and might be away for a few days. I myself pieced out what had happened from stray reports and rumours that trickled out then and later, from what his majesty himself chose to tell me". The old man stopped speaking. After waiting a minute, the young prince's impatience got the better of him.

"And then . . . .", he prompted.

For two days the king and his men had scoured the area, Tara Chand said. Finally, on the third day, they found one of the soldiers. The man had been hideously burnt, but alive. It was as if somebody had tied him to a tree and roasted him. According to his story, he and his companion had spent a few days without encountering anything unusual. And then one night, they had seen what must have been a fire a long distance away. They had immediately set out to investigate it. Upon nearing the source of light, they had proceeded very cautiously.

In spite of the extreme care they had exercised in approaching the little clearing where the light was coming from, they must have been detected; for when they reached it they found it deserted. There was a fire blazing in the centre of the clearing, but of whoever had made it, there was not a trace. As the men stood there, uncertain what to do, there was a furtive movement at the farther edge of the clearing. It was a movement so stealthy, so slight, as to be sensed rather than seen. Uncertain what danger awaited and unable to predict from whither it would come, with their nerves stretched to breaking point under the strain, they made their first fatal error. One of them now unslung the bow he carried and fitting an arrow into it, loosed off a shaft at the spot where the movement had been perceived.

There had been a howl like a wild animal in pain. The men started advancing hesitantly towards the spot—and then it had happened. From another point near the edge of the clearing there was a blinding flash—"It was as if somebody had thrown a lightning bolt at us", said the narrator. "I was blinded and paralysed with searing pain", the man had continued. He had lost consciousness, then.

When he recovered it, it was day. He found himself badly burned and barely able to crawl. "I don't know how I survived for a week", he said. As for his companion, there was not a sign to show what had happened to him. "I could only presume he had died in some horrible fashion. I myself couldn't have lived through another day if your majesty hadn't found me". But search as they would, there was nothing to be learnt about the fate of his companion.

"It seemed that the earth had just opened up and swallowed him", said Tara Chand. The king had finally asked the survivor whether at any time he had been able to catch a glimpse even of who the people were who had started the fire. The man slowly shook his head. "After what I've been through, I can't recall anything quite clearly, your majesty. But from quite far away, it seemed to me I saw a group of children sitting around the fire. But I'm not sure now I didn't dream it".

There was silence now as the tutor stopped speaking. This time the prince, too, seemed too wrapped up in his own thoughts to break it. "But the matter didn't quite end there", said Tara Chand presently. "About a month later, a man from Vithalla had crossed the mountains and gone to the kingdom of Vaishala on the other side. Upon his return, he went straight to the palace and sought audience with the king. On gaining it, he came out with a strange story. He had seen a beggar in the neighbouring kingdom, he said, who looked like the soldier who had gone missing. Upon enquiry he found that the man had appeared there a month earlier, in pitiable condition. He was blind and either could not or would not talk. He hardly moved from where he sat and lived on whatever alms he received from whoever was moved by his pathetic condition. He is so blackened and burned by some terrible fire that if your majesty sees him, you would wonder how he lives", concluded the man.

The king immediately got together three men who had known the missing soldier well and dispatched them on a mission to bring him back if he did indeed turn out to be the man they were looking for. "In a few days the party came back bringing the beggar with them", said Tara Chand. "There was no doubt that it was the missing man". The old man paused and said musingly, "I don't think the king doubted for a moment that once the man had been found, they could get the story of what had happened out of him". But the soldier seemed to have been struck dumb. Indeed it very soon became clear that he had either been robbed off his faculties or was so grievously hurt that he had lost the wit to make any coherent reply, or even understand what was said to him. To every question he either gazed blankly at the questioner or else came out with a vacant, idiot grin. The palace physician had however assured the king that the man could be healed and brought back to his senses. But that was not to be. On the third day after his arrival at Vithalla, the feeble spark of life that had somehow flickered in him, was finally extinguished.

"I must have been a little older than you were when all this happened", said Tara Chand. "It was a lifetime ago and I find it difficult to recall everything very clearly. But I think all this talk of the Mountain Spirits started around then. Some claimed that they were no spirits, but a tribe of dwarfs from the northern regions, who were sorcerers. It was claimed that they avoided humans and anybody who sought to intrude into their reclusive society did so on the pain of being cursed. Whatever they were, after that, I don't think anybody has ever ventured near that region of the hills again".

CHAPTER 11

AN EXCHANGE OF GIFTS

A little breeze sprang up now as the old man ceased talking and ran lightly along the leaves of the tree tops. He got up slowly to his feet. "The cold is reaching my old bones, your majesty. I'll have to go in now", he said. Wordlessly, the boy stood up, cast a long look at the mountains, before slowly following his tutor. They descended a short flight of stairs. Tara Chand lit a taper and by its light reached his cot and stretched himself out on it. He looked at the boy then. "It is getting late for your majesty. You must return to the palace now", he said. The prince nodded absently, then stood still for a minute, regarding the recumbent figure. He then seemed to reach a decision and moved nearer to the cot.

"I was wondering whether you could tell me just one more thing before I go—if you aren't too tired, that is", he added quickly. The old man looked at him questioningly before finally nodding. Thus encouraged, the prince asked:

59

"Was that all there was? The matter ended there and nothing else happened after that?"

The tutor took his time replying, apparently turning over something in his mind. "It wasn't quite the end of the matter, as you've guessed", he said at last. Then, with slow and painful effort, he drew himself up into a sitting position and motioned the young man to draw up a seat near him and sit down. The prince did as he was bidden and waited patiently. "I don't know whether I have a right to tell you any of this", Tara Chand said finally. "If the king, your father, comes to know about it, he may be . . . . displeased, shall we say? I haven't talked about this matter for a very long time and if I'm doing it now, albeit reluctantly, it's principally to keep you from getting a fantastic version of what really happened, from gossip mongering servants or the officious fools you are surrounded by at the palace".

The young man smiled and nodded. "You have my word that whatever you say will be between you and me", he said.

Tara Chand seemed to assay this assurance within himself before proceeding. "In order to make sense of what I'm going to say now, you will have to bear in mind that there has always been an influential obscurantist clique at the palace. I suppose that groups like these are inevitable. I will be more honest than wise, perhaps, when I say that people like these were given less credence under your grandfather, than under your father, the king". The tutor stopped and then continued. "When the time comes for your majesty to ascend the throne, you will have to remember that unless you put these people in their place, it will not take them long to gain ascendancy". There was the beginnings of a smile now on the old man's lips. "And maybe what you hear now will help you to remain alive to the dangers of lending an ear to the counsels of forces such as these".

A month after the incident of the soldier's death, the court astrologer had approached the king. He had had a dream, he said. The Goddess who had watched over the kingdom of Vithalla had appeared in it and told him that She had been gravely displeased by the way the king had dealt with the Mountain Spirits who had been appointed by her to guard the kingdom against invaders from lands beyond the valley. The king must now propitiate these spirits by offering them a suitable tribute. The king, on his part, had listened to this speech with all the deference due to his interlocutor's stature and authority and then sent the astrologer away after promising to think about it.

"I had a feeling that he would have spent the rest of his mortal span duly 'thinking' about it—and done little", said Tara Chand. But it transpired that sometime after the astrologer's visit, the king received a delegation, this time led by the head priest. This worthy had informed the king that there was at large, among the people, a feeling that the slight that had been done to the spirits could be undone only by appeasing them with a special ceremony which, he, the priest, would be willing to perform. Else, the Guardians of the kingdom might very well turn their backs on it, with what disastrous consequences, who can tell.

The king had listened patiently and finally acquiesced. It might not have been the persuasiveness of the priest's entreaty as much as the restiveness of the populace that won the day. But whatever it was, a small figurine of the Goddess was cast in gold; and, after it had been duly consecrated, was taken by the king and a few select courtiers to the mountain clearing which had been the scene of all those stirring events. There, on an auspicious hour, it was solemnly installed, after which the king and his entourage had returned. Upon his majesty's orders, arrangements were made to inspect the clearing every few days to see whether the spirits had indeed accepted the offering.

"Well, the first week passed in expectation that any day the spirits might accept the king's tribute. And then another week passed and then a third. When a whole month had elapsed and the figurine lay untouched in the clearing, the unease started building up. There were murmurs then, rumours of auguries that boded ill for Vithalla and talks of propitiatory sacrifices . . . ." The old man's voice trailed off into silence. "The unease was palpable", he continued. "Every man became a soothsayer. One had seen ravens feeding on a corpse, another had gone to cut wood and seen a tree that had suddenly burst into flames; another, returning late at night, had heard a woman in white sing a mournful dirge". Tara Chand shook his head slowly in wonderment. "The level of hysteria was rising, when one day, the man who had been sent to inspect the clearing had come running back. A huge crowd had gathered outside the palace by the time the king himself came to announce the glad tidings—the figurine had vanished. "The spirits had been propitiated and Vithalla would be spared", said the old man wryly.

"But did it not occur to the king or to anybody else that a golden figurine standing unattended in a mountain top glade could have more likely been stolen, rather than taken away by spirits?" the prince burst out, unable to contain his curiosity any longer.

There was a mischievous gleam in the old man's eyes as he looked at his ward. "Your majesty is a child of your times", he said. "But the fact was, that in the days I'm speaking of, even human cupidity could be subordinated to superstitious awe and nothing less than a royal command could have made any man go near the figurine—or even look at it, for that matter, assuming he could muster the courage to go anywhere near the clearing".

The boy looked thoughtful. "So that was how Vithalla was saved", he said. "But I rather suspect that it is a simpler explanation that it was human agency which was responsible for the vanishing of the icon". He got up now and bowed slowly with folded hands before the other, in ceremonial leave taking for the day. When he straightened, it was to find the old man's eyes fixed on him with an expression he could not quite read.

"I have found your majesty's temper of mind quite gratifyingly close to my own", the tutor said. He sighed then. "It's therefore a pity that the way that affair turned out should so comprehensively disprove that surmise".

The prince's eyes widened. He plumped onto the chair as if his legs had given way under him. "You mean . . . .", he gasped, gaping at Tara Chand. The older man seemed to be enjoying the impression he had created. He nodded slowly. "You haven't heard the last act", he said.

A few months after this incident, some shepherds who had gone near the glade, had seen a peculiar object in the middle of it, said Tara Chand. The frightened shepherds, too terrified to go near it, had promptly informed the king. "His majesty lost no time in investigating this new development. When he reached the clearing early the next day, he found in the centre of it, just as the shepherds had described, a device of some sort. I was in the group of persons who had gone along with the king and saw it for myself". The old man leaned back against his cushion and closed his eyes. He was frowning in recollection now. "Whatever it was, it had been carefully placed on the ground and was knee high. The instrument, or apparatus, or toy . . . . or whatever you want to call it, stood on a small circular metallic plate, to which was fixed an upright metallic shaft. At its upper end was a small solid sphere. And at equally spaced intervals around the middle of this sphere were a number of metal rods, all of which spread out horizontally from the sphere". Tara Chand stopped. The boy waited for him to continue.

"From the end of each of these rods hung a small metallic bead. The beads were of different sizes and seemed to be suspended from very fine silken threads. At least, so it seemed to me". Tara Chand paused to look at the boy. "But to me, the most remarkable thing about the contraption was the metal that had been used in making it. Do you know what it was?"

There was a moment of silence. Then the boy asked softly: "Gold?" There was a brightness in his eyes that the tutor had not seen there before. Tara Chand gave him a long look now. "There are times when I find your majesty's perceptiveness a little intimidating", he said slowly.

CHAPTER 12

"A Curse On My Household And My Kingdom"

"But, as you've guessed, it was all of gold. And of such an exquisite craftsmanship, I don't think I'm going to see the like again. Well, all of us stood around it, looking at it in wonder, trying to think what it could be". The intention behind its appearance there, at least, seemed clear enough to everybody gathered there. The king's gesture had been reciprocated. And there were those who thought that by that reciprocation, maybe the spirits were making it clear that the king had indeed made amends for whatever slight he had unwittingly offered.

"So ran our thoughts. All this time, the little glade had remained in the shadow of the tall circle of trees that fringed it. Meanwhile, the sun had been rising steadily and now, topping the branches of the tallest trees, suddenly lit up the little clearing in a burst of brilliant light, so that what had been a leafy cavern, now lay bathed in that light like an opened jewel casket".

And then a wonderful thing had happened. As the knot of people who were standing around the device watched in amazement, the upper plate, with its rods and silken threads from which hung the beads, began to spin around—slowly at first and then with increasing speed, till it was merrily whirling with such rapidity, that the beads were almost on a level with the rods from which they were suspended. At that, a good part of the watching throng had taken to their heels at the exhibition of this spectral power of a ghostly hand. But to many of the braver ones who had stayed to watch this curious spectacle, a thought had come almost at the same time. It was the custom in those times, to tie to the cradle of infants, small metal or wooden discs, from whose edge would be suspended little coloured beads—or even pebbles with those who could not afford the beads. The contraption could be twirled around by the hand, or by the wind when it passed over it. There was not a shadow of doubt in the minds of many of us that this marvelous toy had been bestowed on the king as a gift to his one year old infant son.

"And so we reverently carried it back. As we did, we noticed something else. Whenever the device came into the shadow, it stopped spinning. It seemed to gather some mysterious force from the sun".

For two days the device was kept outside the palace so that the people of Vithalla could see how their king had been favoured by the Spirits. "I rather suspect the priest to have been behind that bit of display", said Tara Chand. "He lost no opportunity to tell anybody who would care to listen to him, how he had appeased the Mountain Spirits through his ceremonies, thereby delivering Vithalla from the catastrophic visitation of their wrath. And there were quite a few who were impressed by these claims. After all, had not the Spirits bestowed their blessings on the infant prince with this wondrous adornment?" The tutor stopped as a small sound came from the direction of the door of the chamber.

"Who's there?" called out the old man. One of the two men who accompanied the prince whenever he left the palace, entered respectfully and bowed to them before addressing the prince.

"It is getting late, your majesty", he said. "The king has issued strict orders that your majesty should be in the palace before the moon enters the second quarter".

The prince appeared torn between the filial injunction and his curiosity to hear the story. He turned pleadingly to the tutor. "Oh, please. Can I stay a little longer? Surely you can tell the king no harm would come of it if I return a little later than usual one day?"

Tara Chand saw the entreaty in the boy's face and turned to the guard. "Go out and wait. He will be with you shortly". The guard bowed again and left.

"Tell me now", said the boy. "What happened to the miracle machine?"

"It's curious you should call it that", said Tara Chand. "But there isn't much more to say. I remember thinking later, however, that the king had expressed almost no opinion in the matter". He stopped again, then continued. "Your grandsire was a rare king. Though he did not hesitate to consult others, he kept his own counsel. And his opinion on most matters was generally sound".

At the end of the two days, the device was carried in and hung above the infant prince's cot. Being very heavy, it was hung from strong ropes attached to the ceiling. And during the day, sometimes, the sunlight would be reflected on to it by polished metal plates. It would then start spinning again and its lustre would fill that room. Kings from neighbouring kingdoms, who had heard of it had come to see it. Nobody who saw it would easily forget it". The shawl that Tara Chand had wrapped around himself had slipped from his shoulders. He now drew it around himself and readjusted it to his satisfaction.

"Whatever the device was, it exercised a fascination over me I found difficult to resist. I used to go to the palace every day to look at it. But the more I saw it, the more the uneasy feeling within me grew that all of us had failed to understand the real purpose of that strange toy. Sometimes, as I stood watching it as it spun noiselessly in the reflected sunlight, a thing of exquisitely iridescent beauty, a half formed thought would rise within me". Tara Chand stopped now, groping for words. "Maybe I had seen something like it somewhere; or maybe it was merely a fleeting wisp of an idea that the contraption was meant to suggest. But whatever it was, ironically, it brought little comfort to the prince who lay under it all day. For, I don't think the young prince, your uncle, had much opportunity to enjoy it. Exactly a month after the cradle adornment had been hung up in his bedchamber, the infant prince was dead".

They were days when life was a fragile gift. Two brief and burning days of fever was all it took to bereave a king and snatch an heir from a throne. The king, never

69

one to give way to his emotions, was yet inconsolable. "'That wretched bauble is a curse on my household and my kingdom', I remember his telling me one day. I think that by that time he was coming around to accepting the presence of the Mountain Spirits and their malign designs against him and his kingdom. In such wise do the events of our life unman the strongest and the most resolute of men". Tara Chand paused. "Not that I would blame him entirely. For, in the few years that followed, Vithalla entered upon a period of calamitous misfortune that was unrivalled in living memory. There were years of pestilences, famines, drought and flood. That may have been one reason why the Spirits and their doings failed to engage public attention. Nothing more was heard about them after that—and nor did anybody venture near that haunted glade again. Finally, when the murmurs had started running round the exhausted populace of a mass migration from the region, the years of ordeal mercifully came to a close. And, surprising as it may seem now, nobody during all those years could summon the courage to bring up with the king the matter of the Spirits and their appeasement. It was a few years after that, that your father, the king was born".

As the narration came to a close, the old man leaned back gratefully from the exertion and closed his eyes. Neither spoke for a minute or two. The tutor finally opened his eyes and looked at his ward. "It is getting late for your highness", he reminded gently. "You must leave now". The boy nodded slowly, stood up and bowed respectfully for the second time that night. He started leaving the room, but barely had he reached the door, when he came back again.

"There is just one thing I would request you to tell me". Tara Chand nodded. "What happened to that wonder toy?"

Tara Chand seemed to take his time replying. "After the death of his son, the king ordered that it should be taken down and put away somewhere out of sight. There was some talk later, of taking it back to the mountain top and leaving it there. But to my knowledge, that was never done. In fact, I don't think anybody saw it again after that—except the person it finally reached".

"So there was somebody who finally took it?" asked the boy with quickening interest. The older man merely shrugged indifferently. "You see, even then, I suppose there were people whose greed for gold was strong enough to overcome superstitious dread of what the king himself had described as 'a wretched bauble'—some fawning and covetous courtier, maybe, or some member of the royal household who was close to the king—who knows?"

"Oh", said the boy thoughtfully. "I thought . . . .", he did not complete the sentence and shook his head as if to rid himself of some persistent notion. "Whoever got it, I can't believe that was the motive—or at least, maybe not the whole motive". He added as an afterthought, then: "I think I would like to find out what happened to it".

The tutor sat up in his cot now. "I earnestly implore your majesty not to engage upon such an enterprise", he said. "There are certain things which are beyond our understanding at present. And it is not wisdom to enquire too deeply into these things".

The unwonted vehemence of the old tutor and his entreaty which went so much against the grain of his own oft repeated principle that truth would never cause permanent harm and no excuse should be used to stifle enquiry, took the young man aback. However, on regaining his composure, he replied placatingly enough: "I certainly will not do it, if you don't want me to. But do you believe, as my grandfather seems to have done, that the gift came with a family curse from the Spirits?"

"I don't know what to believe", came the reply. "I will therefore content myself with this observation. It is extremely doubtful you will find anything after all these years. But even if you do not find anything, even if the fact of your being engaged upon this quest were to reach the ears of the king, it would be difficult to predict what his response would be". After a pause he continued: "As your majesty grows older, you will realize that living in a society like ours carries certain constraints, one of which is that you don't always embark on a venture even if you are convinced of the rightness of it. In fact, you will realise this to be a fundamental principle of statecraft".

Long after the prince had gone, Tara Chand sat on his cot in the darkness, staring into vacancy. He heard the housekeeper close and latch the front door and retire to his quarters for the night. He fell into a light doze then and on coming out of it, guessed the hour well past midnight. He must have been woken up by the night patrol going on their rounds. He had been dreaming. He was carrying the golden device, all alone, to the mountain top and on reaching it, had kept it there, relief flooding his heart and mind. Suddenly, there were children there—they were gazing at him silently. Unable to bear that eerie scrutiny, he had turned and hurried away from the clearing. He had heard the sound of pursuit then and had started running . . . . running . . . .

The old tutor got up slowly and unsteadily to his feet. He moved carefully in the dark to an adjoining chamber where a wick was burning in a small earthen lamp. He looked for a taper, found one, lit it and carrying it, moved to a small antechamber. Upon entering it, he turned to latch it behind him. The room had the musty smell of neglected odds and ends accumulated over a long lifetime. Tara Chand went to the farther corner of it now, sat down on the floor and carefully placed the taper on the ground beside him. He began feeling sections of the wall gropingly. Finally, finding whatever he had been looking for, he pressed his finger tips to the wall with increasing pressure, pushing it to one side. Suddenly a panel slid back with a small squeak, to reveal a small, cunningly designed alcove behind it. Tara Chand looked around him, then took up the taper with hands that shook a little, moved it to the tenebrous recess that the panel had revealed and peered into its dark interior.

CHAPTER 13

MASTER AND PUPIL

As the understanding between the tutor and his young ward grew, it was only natural that under the influence of the rapport thus established, the former should begin to depart increasingly from the narrow responsibilities of formal instruction that would normally have been his proper domain. He began to take the prince out on brief excursions to show him his people and how they lived. On these occasions, they travelled incognito, assuming the coarse cloth habit worn by the common people. The whole exercise was rendered easier by the fact that owing to his reticence, the prince had avoided participation in public ceremonies and there was, in consequence, none to recognize him when he set forth on such outings.

"Many years ago there lived a prince like yourself, in a kingdom to the North", he told his student once. "His father, the king, wishing to spare him the travails of an earthly existence and the ultimate terrifying mystery called death, did everything he could to shield his son from the sight of human suffering. But it failed signally. The knowledge, when it did come to the prince, devastated him so much that he left his people, his wife, his child and his throne and went into the world to seek human sorrow, to know it and finally find a way of ending it. I think it's better for you to see it for yourself now. You have wisdom enough to use your experience in the service of your people".

And so the prince, accompanied by his preceptor, went to places where no royal foot had trodden before. And he observed. But, unlike prince Siddhartha, if he felt seared by the appalling horror of what he had seen, he betrayed no visible sign of it. It made old Tara Chand himself uneasy—the unmoving calmness with which the young man saw the terrible conditions under which his subjects lived. So that he would sometimes ask himself whether he had erred in his assessment of the prince's personality. Under the circumstances, it was a bit unfair that he would not live to see what the spectacle of suffering, on the scale he had been able to show the prince, had done to transform him.

But whatever doubts he had, vanished when he introduced the boy to a study of the science of the day—especially astronomy and mathematics. It did not take the avid young student long to exhaust what his teacher could tell him. When he pressed Tara Chand about where he could find more about these fields, the older man had an idea. "You'll go to Nalanda", he declared one day. "That is the only place for you". Nalanda, in those days, was the greatest university in the world, enjoying the patronage of mighty emperors and holding its own as a dazzling international centre for study and research in the sciences and metaphysics.

He duly sought royal permission for the excursion and obtained it with some skilful persuasion. For, it puzzled the king why anybody should want to go so far away (he had not heard of the place himself) to acquaint himself with the mystic properties of strange cabalistic figures like triangles and circles (for in such terms did he insist on understanding the noble hieroglyphics of geometry) when the court astrologer could have taught all these any day to him. And, as for the prince's interest in astronomy, were not the stars plainly visible at night? Of what avail was it to learn their names in Sanskrit? Would it help one to follow their celestial gyrations better to determine the most auspicious hour for sacrifices or the seasons for feasts and fasts? The tutor handled his sovereign's petulant queries with tact and craved royal indulgence for his ward's unusual preoccupations. "If your Majesty will grant the young prince this favour, I will assure you that you will find him more willing to take up his royal duties on his return".

In touching upon this matter of the prince's strange disinclination to participate in royal ceremonials, Tara Chand was, of course, taking a calculated risk. For, the position was somewhat like this. The heir to Vithalla's throne was a young man eighteen years of age, while his brother was seven years younger. The latter had already established himself as a palace favourite, excelling in the more boisterous activities that came to him as the privilege of his position. He was a strapping lad who showed every inclination to savour whatever good the world had to offer; while in this he was hardly any different from gilded youth through the long millennia of human social existence, his exalted position afforded him opportunities that were rarely available to the average youngster of his day. Against this exuberance, the pensive gentleness of the elder stood in unfavourable contrast. He was an indifferent horseman, for instance, and at the royal hunts tended to quietly lag behind and after the din had faded in the air, dismount and walk back as unobtrusively as he could to his tent in the camp. If this were not bad enough, the reek of the blood and slaughter of the hunt nauseated him and in the evening, before the hunters returned, he would be ensconced in his room at the palace. It was unfortunately not an age that valued such sensitivities and of late the king had become increasingly embarrassed by what he perceived to be a certain lack of manly qualities in his elder son.

When the royal brow furrowed, Tara Chand decided he had gone too far. But he was agreeably surprised when the king, after a moment of quiet thought, assented. The teacher immediately sought out his pupil and conveyed the welcome tidings to him. That night the prince dined by invitation at the former's house. "I have influential friends who will be able to help you on the way", said Tara Chand. Then he described to his student the way he should take and the geography of the regions he would encounter. "It's best you embark on your journey as soon as you can. It's difficult to say what may happen if you allow the king too much time to think over this project of yours. You must know there are interests working against you in your father's kingdom", he added slowly.

"That's surprising", replied his interlocutor in genuine astonishment. "What could I have done to earn this enmity?"

"It may not be so much what you did as all the things you did not do", rejoined his teacher a little cryptically. "It will be useful to bear this in mind whatever you do". The prince nodded. "I've decided to leave early day after tomorrow morning, anyway".

True to his word, the next day itself he put together the few things that he would need to take with him. Finally came all the farewells. That night he went to take leave of the old teacher. "I knew you would be ready by evening", the latter said. "There are few preparations to be made when your journey is going to be very long or very short. And there is none to be made for the last and longest journey of all".

"True", said the young man. "And who may know whether I begin mine tomorrow".

The old man did not speak immediately. "I do not think so", he said finally. "But I will enjoin you to bear in mind that your life is no longer yours entirely, to do what you want with it". He was silent for a moment. "You've seen the condition of life of your people. You are the only one capable of doing anything to lift them out of that misery". He held up a hand sensing the other beginning to say something. "Hear me out. There is not much time". The old man seemed to be husbanding his strength carefully. "I know that the solution to this problem should begin with men's attitudes". The teacher fell silent again, before continuing. "We need a king who is capable of believing that his destiny is not compassed within the dissolute decadence of hunting, drinking, dallying with courtesans and engagement in an occasional war.

"Remember that this excursion to Nalanda and back is the last indulgence that will be allowed to you as a private citizen, Ram Pal". The young prince's name slipped out easily for the first and last time out of his teacher's mouth. "When I won the permission for it from your royal father, His Majesty, I promised him that on your return you will be willing to take up your responsibilities as the prince who will one day ascend the throne. When I gave him that assurance, he had no right to know that, when I talked about your responsibilities, I had weightier things in mind than the tedious silliness of palace ceremonies. You will have to remember who you are, my son and so resolve never to set yourself a private objective that would be higher than the welfare of your people. I do not have to say anything more than that". The effort of that long talk was telling on the old man now. He paused to get his breath back. The young man had waited patiently, without saying a word. He now leaned forward to arrange the cushions behind the old man's back. He sat there for half an hour. Complete silence reigned between the two. Finally, the prince rose, bowed and reverently touched his teacher's feet. The old man raised both hands in blessing. That was the last farewell.

CHAPTER 14

NALANDA

By the time the sun had risen the next morning, the prince had left Vithalla behind him. He knew the general direction in which his destination lay. But it was another matter to take a direct bearing towards it, in a region where lofty and mountainous ramparts hid the land that lay beyond. But when you are young and in excellent health and have, moreover, turned your face towards a destination which is filled with beguiling possibilities, the privations of the way cannot bother you. Indeed, the journey itself brought such newness every day in terms not merely of the changing landscape, but of the variety of the cultures and convenances of the regions he passed through, its heady novelty was like a wine to the young prince. As he took a deep draught of it, he wondered whether anything Nalanda had to offer would compare with the delights of the journey itself. There finally came a day when that doubt could be settled.

The prince stood in awe before the colossal walls of the university buildings. As he walked around the library, he realized that it was many times larger than the palace he had lived in. He was astonished to learn that the library contained over a million volumes. There were huge monasteries, temples, dormitories for the monks and students. In the last stage of the journey, he had been accompanied by a guide that a friend of Tara Chand had arranged for him. The eager young prince conducted his enquiries through him now. Seeing several large halls, he enquired now about what purpose they served. His awe turned to wonder when he was informed that they were lecture halls. He had been told that there were thousands of students and teachers who lived there and learned and taught. When he had doubted whether the account owed anything to exaggeration, the vastness of the domestic quarters left him in no doubt about the populousness of the university. There were foreigners too from as far away as China and Korea. Nalanda, at that point of time, was a flourishing centre where Buddhist philosophy was taught and researched. In fact, it was associated with the name of the Buddha himself. The great teacher had stayed many times and had often preached in its vicinity.

Nor was it to be thought that the scholars of Nalanda allowed their interests to be circumscribed by metaphysics. Aryabhatta himself had studied there five hundred years ago and his mathematics and astronomy were still taught. As also were the great astronomical theories of Varamihira and the towering Brahmagupta, the greatest astronomer of the world of his day. They had carried astronomy to the farthest point it could be taken to without the use of telescopes.

Within a year the prince had mastered the language sufficiently to be able to read and from then on his progress proceeded apace. The young man read avidly everything that came his way—the science and mathematics of the day and even the theories of linguistic morphology of the great grammarian Panini. But without a doubt, his special love was astronomy. Through many a long night did he lie on his back, looking at the crowded splendour of the night sky and wondering at the law that kept those lights moving in their orderly and convoluted cavalcade. How many of those harboured intelligences, he asked himself. And sometimes his mind would drift towards the maker of the law and the One who sustained those countless millions of celestial lights and kept them on their course and on Earth, the whole panoply of created Life. It was a season for such speculation. There was an innocence about that wakening wonder which still deserved that name. Ram Pal of Vithalla could perhaps be forgiven for not realising that he was living in a privileged age. For, if the succeeding centuries loosed a torrent of knowledge of the world and its environs, and of the universe itself, they also insisted on classifying, and in the process fragmenting speculation itself into first, one or other schools of metaphysics and philosophy; and then into religion; and finally into denominations of them, with a sectarian thoroughness that finally killed the greatest cerebral enterprise that the human mind could undertake, by smothering the freshness of that enquiry.

Through all this, it is true that Vithalla and its affairs were always present in the young prince's mind. If these memories were not edged with the poignance of experienced immediacy, they nevertheless claimed a large part of his waking moments, even in surroundings which had so much to offer to one of a speculative cast of mind. For what Nalanda offered, beyond a knowledge structure that could inspire wonder, was a chance to interact with the representatives of a culture that was as different as could be from that of his faraway Himalayan realm. For the winds of the world blew through the place.

And the young, ever in the vanguard of change and acting as its great standard bearers, were impatiently trying their best to turn that wind into a gale. They saw little reason to continue to live under values and beliefs—and most importantly, restraints—that had shaped a past of which most of them had seen less than two decades, anyway. As with all reformers impatient for change, if they had been shown the contours of the world they were longing to unveil, it is doubtful how many of them would have continued to seek it. But debate is a salutary exercise; and of that commodity, none could complain about a shortage there.

Almost alone among all those young scholars who jostled and thronged through the halls of Nalanda, the prince of Vithalla was in a position of one whose privilege had set him above the necessity of having to work for a living. Wisely then, he did nothing to betray the exaltedness of that social station and on the other hand, adapted to the rigours of a monastic existence almost with relief. If he lacked a monk's self-flagellating humility and was human enough to feel the washing of clothes and the performance of menial tasks through which he was expected to earn his keep, an irksome obligation, he accepted it willingly enough as part of a communal existence that had no place in it for the privileges of rank and position. In an important sense, it came, therefore, as a completion of the inculcation of egalitarian values that Tara Chand had begun.

There was another reason that made such obligations easier to bear. There was an air at the university, especially among its younger members, that militated against all hereditary privilege. Privilege had to be earned, merited—to come upon it in any other way was to prey upon those who really deserved it. With the naïve self-interest that is at the bases of all revolutionary positions, it did not occur to them to enquire from where the resource had come to set up the university and how much any of them had contributed to—and thereby earned the right to benefit from—its continued existence; or, for that matter, how much of what they were receiving went back to the social institutions that maintained the university and its higher learning. But, by a curious irony, this inability to look at their own privileged position in no way lessened the force of an opposition to another's. The result was the almost passionate, and on occasion militant espousal of the ideals which a later age would have called republicanism. Hereditary monarchies were still the rule the world over. But if the world had allowed the younger members of Nalanda to legislate on its behalf, their majesties and highnesses would have got short shrift. The prince of Vithalla had already been prepared for these doctrines by temper and training, and so it was that they found ready lodgment in his receptive mind.

He became particularly close to two young teenaged students from Korea. Tham and his sister had belonged to an affluent family and like himself had sought out faraway Nalanda, after exhausting everything their tutors could teach them. Though younger than the prince, Tham was much more worldly wise with a penetratingly shrewd insight into human nature. On occasion he had used these traits to ease, for the prince, any difficulty against which his more meditative and reticent nature might have proved unequal.

One day, after he had been there for four years, a stranger came seeking him, to the cell he shared with two other students. He was from a province neighbouring Vithalla. Upon learning that he would be visiting this part of the country, Vithalla's king had asked him to carry a letter to his son.

It had been written on a rough, parchment like cloth, with berry juice serving as ink. The sheet had been rolled up and cased in a bamboo tube sealed at one end with wax. The prince opened it with a heart that was beating fast. It was not easy to read the clumsily indited epistle, with the ink smudged at places and the material itself suffering inevitable damage in the process of its journey.

A merciful God had seen fit to preserve the king and queen and the other members of the royal household in reasonably good health, the king had written. However, his teacher Tara Chand had passed away a few days after his departure. The king then moved on to the subject of his younger son. His younger brother, prince Lakkan Pal, had now grown into a fine young man. "You would not recognize him", the king said. He was as strong as two men and had already distinguished himself in several wrestling tournaments. "He has made his people, the court and his parents proud with these manly achievements", the king declared. The prince smiled at the implicit rebuke. The letter went on to say that the king hoped that he (the prince) was profiting from his labours at Nalanda. Further, the queen joined the king in wishing that he would be able to return soon to assume his royal responsibilities.

And so the days and months and years flew past. And three more years went. And at the end of that time, the young prince finally realised that he no longer had any compelling reasons to remain at the university. While it was true that he could become more expert in any discipline that he found worthy of study, the acquisition of such expertise was too narrow to significantly push back his horizon. And so, with a sigh, he decided one day that the time had come to leave Nalanda. As soon as he had arrived at the decision, he wasted no time in translating it into action. Exactly as he had done seven years ago when leaving Vithalla, his preparations were made in the next day, and by the end of it, all his farewells said—a procedure that was rendered easier by the fact that he had few friends and virtually no intimates.

CHAPTER 15

RETURN TO VITHALLA

Early on the morning of the following day, he turned his back on the university. He decided that a chapter of his life was closing, with a finality which would admit of no return and that he was going towards an uncertain future that offered little in compensation for what he was leaving behind. During that long journey back, that realisation would fill him with desperation and he would have to muster all his resolution sometimes, to continue on his course, instead of abandoning it to return to Nalanda. But he plodded on, raising one foot and putting it before the other, with weary repetition, conscious that with each such act he was drawing nearer to Vithalla. Finally, one evening, he topped the last rise and saw below him the long valley, like a crease on the fabric of the Earth from this height, that contained his kingdom. He had reached the little clearing that had played such a momentous role in the fortunes of his country and stayed there that night, reluctant to go on any further. He gazed long and wonderingly as he had done so many times, at the night sky, before he fell asleep.

The next morning he started the descent to the floor of the valley. To his relief, when he reached the city, he found that there was none to recognize the person who had left seven years ago. The palace was, however, agog at the return of their young prince. After he had paid his devoirs to God at the palace temple for bringing him back safely, he was led to the king's chamber, where he was received by his parents with a warmth that touched him. He became a little ashamed, then, when he remembered the unwillingness with which he had returned to his kingdom. His younger brother came to see him, finally. Prince Lakkan Pal was a fine specimen of manhood—tall and powerfully built and with the striking good looks he had obviously inherited from his mother's side. The letter had not exaggerated the young prince's winsomeness, he decided.

The king spoke now. "Your tutor Tara Chand had drawn up a will, bequeathing everything he owned to you", he said. The old tutor had been childless and under the prevailing law, with no surviving siblings or legal heirs to claim his estate, it would normally have lapsed to the state. But Tara Chand, being a member of the royal family, had the right to nominate an heir. "It seemed he had also specifically directed that a rather heavy wooden box in his possession should be carried to your chamber and left there. The will mentions that it should be opened by none but you", said the king. "Whatever it was inside, it must have been very heavy", continued the king. "I'm told it took four strong men to lift it".

As soon as he could leave the royal presence, the prince hurried to his chamber, his heart beating fast. When he reached it, he closed the door behind him and carefully secured it from the inside. The box had been placed under his bed. With tremendous effort he pulled it out and then saw to his astonishment that the seal of the royal household had been set upon it. He knew that for anyone who was not the designated person to break the seal, even accidentally, attracted a death penalty. He broke it now, certainty flooding him as he did so, what he would find inside. The massive lid creaked as he removed it and was carefully placed on the ground.

Hardly daring to breathe now, he removed layer upon layer of old musty smelling cloth. When the last layer came away, he caught his breath as he looked at the wondrous object that stood revealed; he did not have the shadow of a doubt in his mind that he was looking at the golden bauble, that according to his grandfather, had come as a curse on his country and his household. For a few minutes, he could not take his eyes off it. And then he saw the tightly wound scroll of parchment that was at the bottom of the box. He took it up immediately and opened it. It was a letter from Tara Chand.

My son,

I am finally taking the liberty of addressing you thus. Indeed, by the time you read this, I would have been released from all obligations of observing any earthly ceremonies, not to talk of merely royal ones. I am afraid, in this matter—as on almost any other—your father would not agree with me. It would therefore be best if the knowledge of this letter and its contents were to remain with you. I would like to relate briefly how I came into the possession of what you will find in this box.

During the calamitous years that followed the death of your grandsire's son, he could not bring himself to look at this gift from the Spirits. At that time, I had enjoyed a privileged position in the royal household as a close confidant of the king and I used the strength of that connection now, to make a request. I told the king of the fascination the toy exercised over me and my belief that it had a purpose which went beyond being hung up as a cradle ornament—that, in fact, it was vitally necessary for us to understand what that purpose was. I had no difficulty in persuading his majesty to allow me to take custody of it. It was an arrangement that remained between the king and myself; the confidentiality of the entire procedure being made easier by the fact that there was none who dared to enquire about the fate of that golden curse. So that, after it came into my hands, it dropped out of the royal household's memory.

Such being the circumstances of my acquisition, you will understand my extreme reservation about the disclosure of it. This is especially so since there is a gulf between his majesty, your father's temperament and mine on matters of this sort. As I have already explained to you, it would have been difficult to predict how he would have reacted to the disclosure.

For some time now I have entertained a suspicion about what the device really is. It is a notion so fantastic that I will not advance it here. Besides, with your greater astuteness, knowledge and the variety of intellectual resources which you have acquired at Nalanda, you will surely penetrate to whatever is the truth behind it. I have nothing more to say. I will therefore take this last opportunity to remind you of your destiny, especially in the larger historical context of the deliverance of your people.

The prince closed his eyes and sat still in his bed. What was it that the old tutor had suspected the toy to be that he found too outrageous to communicate? Twice more did he read the epistle, more slowly and more carefully each time. Was it something that Tara Chand could have imagined, he asked himself. After all one could not live a long lifetime in a culture of superstitious dread, among a people who tended to personify any force that they did not understand and invest Nature with human lineament and design, without finally allowing it to leach into one's soul.

The young man was gazing absently out of the window at the prospect outside, as his thoughts ran thus, when his attention was suddenly attracted by a small sound. He turned around quickly and was amazed at what he saw. He found that the sun rays coming in through the window had reached the device. Under the influence of that mysterious power, the toy had begun spinning, much as Tara Chand had described. It was an iridescent, whirling wonder now and the prince watched it in fascination. He could understand the spell it had cast on Tara Chand. As he watched, the contraption began to spin faster and faster and the golden beads flashed in the sun, like damsels around a maypole. Faster and faster, faster and faster it got.

Suddenly something jogged loose in his memory, something that he had heard of often enough at Nalanda. The shock of his discovery petrified him, so that he gaped at the whirling marvel, forgetting to blink and even breathe. Blinding illumination flooded his mind instantly as he realised what the toy was and why it had been given.

CHAPTER 16

A PARENTAL CONCLAVE

The next few days that followed were spent in tranquil inactivity. He knew that it was a period of grace, to allow him to take up the threads of palace existence again. And this the prince conscientiously tried to do. It became sometimes an overwhelming temptation to wall himself up against the siege of the tedium bred by the elaborately codified trivialities of palace ceremonials. But, while resolutely resisting it, he decided it would be best for everybody if he were to engage with the thousand and one palace duties no more than was strictly necessary. He was agreeably surprised to find this indulgence granted to him. A few days later, however, he found that it came with a cost. On that morning, he was told that the king was waiting for him in his chamber and wished to talk to him. Rather to his surprise, he found that it was to be a private audience with his parents. This presaged that the king had matters of moment in his mind and the young man could not help wondering uneasily what was coming as he took his seat. In the event, his father did not keep him waiting for long.

"When Tara Chand sought from me the permission for you to go Nalanda", began the king directly, "he gave me his word that upon your return you would willingly take up the duties for which God has ordained you". There was a little silence now and the prince's heart sank within him. "He assured me further that he would talk to you himself and make it plain to you the condition under which you would be allowed to go", the king continued and looked keenly at him.

The latter nodded. "I had no intention of reneging on that conditionality, sire", he replied firmly.

"That is good, my son. I will continue on that understanding, then. It must not have escaped your notice that you are already at an age when young men in your position have assumed the responsibilities of a householder and have begotten children". The king stopped and looked at his son, trying to gauge his reaction. But the customary expressionless serenity of his son's face gave nothing away. "Accordingly, the queen—your mother—and I have decided that it is time we found for you a bride who would be a fitting wife for you and a daughter-in-law to us and no less importantly, one who deserves to sit by your side on the throne of this country, on the day it becomes yours".

The queen, who had been silent all this while, spoke now. "Indeed, my son, even while you were away pursuing your studies, we had initiated this process and have chosen three princesses of neighbouring kingdoms. Careful enquiries have established beyond doubt that they are young women of steadfast virtue and fully befitted to be welcomed into a royal house like ours. It has been our devout hope that you would select one of them as your consort-to-be". It was the queen's turn to look anxiously at her son. As we have seen, she had never understood him completely, and at this point of time was even more uncertain than formerly about his attitudes.

The prince sighed. It was a move that he had been expecting. He had seen and heard enough of palace life to have more than a reasonably good understanding of the sort of life that awaited him as a "householder". He found the prospect unattractive. It was not that he was against marriage itself. If he had had the freedom, he would have married a woman who was a commoner, as his own mother had been. But what he had seen of princesses did not encourage the belief that he could happily spend the remainder of his life with one of them. He conjured up in his mind's eye the vision of the last one that had come to stay at the palace, before his departure to Nalanda. He had suspected that his parents had hoped that she would have found favour in his eyes. Accordingly, every opportunity was found to discreetly leave the young people in each other's company.

He found her a plump and cheerful creature, with an uncomplicated view of life. One day, the queen had suggested that he should show their royal guest around the palace garden, after lunch. But it was not till evening that he could go to the garden. He found her eating fruit and spitting the stones out explosively. As he watched interestedly, she explained that she was trying to see how far she could make the seed go. "One went over there", she said pointing with a chubby and beringed finger to the foot of a gigantic peepul tree that stood in massive majesty, apparently unruffled by this indignity.

"That is wonderful", the prince had said politely.

She turned to him then. "Do you know I've been waiting here all afternoon for you?", she asked petulantly.

"I'm sorry", the prince apologised. "Actually I would have been here earlier, but my tutor wouldn't let me go", he explained.

The princess popped another berry into her mouth without answering, chewed it into pulp and followed it with another burst of breath and another launch. She carefully noted the place where it came to rest and seemed disappointed with the result. "So your tutor detained you". She paused a minute, lost in thought. "You must have him whipped", she said finally.

"Eh?", said the prince, jolted out of his composure, wondering if this was some ununderstood variety of sophisticated jest.

"I said you must have your tutor whipped. If you don't, they start getting above themselves. I have mine whipped once in about two months, you know. He'd become impossible otherwise".

The prince imagined old Tara Chand being whipped and was secretly amused.

"I see you don't like your tutor much", he said, at loss for a better reply.

The princess pouted her lips. "He makes me do all sorts of silly things".

"Like what?", he enquired, his curiosity aroused.

"Well, he asked me once that if there were seven baskets, each one having fifteen berries, how many berries there were in all".

"And what did you do?" he asked.

"I told him if I wanted to know things like that, I can ask my maid".

He thought over this answer. "That's true. But what if she doesn't know how to count?"

The princess did not reply immediately, being pre-occupied with the task of choosing a berry more luscious and sweeter than the rest. Finally she made her choice and pushed it into her mouth. As he watched fascinatedly, the explosive ejection followed once again. The performance was apparently more satisfactory this time, bringing a smile of approval to her face. She addressed his question now. "What if she doesn't know how to count?", she echoed. "Well, he could teach her then".

He had to concede the reasonableness of the solution.

He found out that princess Namita lived for two things: Food and clothes. The palace and state ceremonials she looked forward to as occasions when she could indulge these twin preoccupations. She had also complained to him about the lax ways of the palace staff at Vithalla. "We would never allow that', she told him.

He had nodded understandingly. "Some whipping is certainly in order", he told her.

But irony was lost on the young lady. "I'll attend to all that when we're married", she assured him archly. The prince quaked inwardly. Fortunately for him, he had been delivered from the necessity of having to communicate his decision to decline the honour of her hand, by Tara

Chand's sudden decision to send him to Nalanda and the train of events that had followed.

The prince cleared his throat. He looked at the queen now. "I cannot thank you enough for all the effort you are making to secure my happiness. I have been thinking about the matter of late". He paused. "Sometimes, when I think of where my mother came from, I feel . . ." The queen was looking at him with a little frown of perplexment. "Feel what, my son?", she prompted encouragingly.

He plucked up courage at this. "Why, I was wondering that, considering my own background, it would perhaps be more suitable if I were to marry a woman of the people". The royal countenances registered shock and dismay.

"You have returned from . . . . that . . . that place where you'd gone to study, with some strange ideas. I shouldn't have allowed myself to be persuaded by Tara Chand into sending you there. Is that what they teach you there? You are a king's son now and can no longer think of going where your inclination takes you, remember. You have a duty to fulfil to your people". Since this was almost an echo of what Tara Chand had told him before he had left for Nalanda, though in a very different context, the prince was impressed in spite of himself.

The king now used what he considered to be his decisive argument. "Would you say also that since you were a commoner, you would like to give up the throne?" The prince desisted from telling his father that that was precisely what he would like to do if he had the choice. In fact, it had been the shadow of an idea he had been toying with after his return. Why not renounce the throne in favour of his younger brother? It was an idea that had come to him at Nalanda and if he did not immediately express it, it was because he saw compelling reasons against it.

He had been appalled by the conditions under which most of his subjects lived and had accepted unreservedly Tara Chand's injunction that he should accept the responsibility of amelioration of those conditions as nothing less than a divine trust. He knew it was a task that meant no less than a resolve to confront the powerful forces of stasis; for the empowerment of the people, it was a necessary pre-condition that there should be a progressive diminution in authority a hereditary nobility wielded over them. It was a monumental task, Tara Chand had assured him and could be undertaken only by one for whom the power over men that kingship conferred held no attractions in itself. In his idler moments he had wondered whether the old teacher had sent him to Nalanda to prepare him for just this responsibility. But he knew he lacked the revolutionary fervour of many of the young men he had come across at the university. He knew also that he lacked the vital energies that leadership demanded—the ability to communicate effectively with men, to mobilize them with emotional arguments and finally to fire them with ideals under whose ardour they would allow themselves to be converted into factors in a situation. A detachment bred of a contemplative turn of mind had made it difficult for him to get carried away by millennial messages. If he had to work within his limitations, he knew that the reformation of the old order had to be achieved through gradual marches rather than by a headlong storming of its citadels. On the plane of policy, it meant a transformation of existing institutions, rather than a sweeping of them into limbo.

He had thought about these things, then, and had reached certain provisional conclusions. He was realistic enough to doubt whether such speculations could constitute even an outline for action—but he was still able to derive from them a crumb of comfort that kingship could have its compensations in the power they invested in him to allay the misery of a people crushed under the iron heel of an indifferent Nature and a monarchy which existed only to prey on them. There was none, of course, with whom he could have discussed these ideas. He had hoped that his old tutor would have lived long enough, if not to guide him along this path, at least to set him on it. But since that was not be, he had carefully kept these reflections to himself during the long years at Nalanda.

It was with relief, therefore, that he addressed the subject of his accession to the throne. If for nothing else than that, it would allow him to deflect attention from a discussion of his matrimonial intentions. Accordingly, he made answer now. "I know any plans that both of you have made for me would have nothing else than my welfare as its object. However, I thought that where the commonweal was involved, I could draw a distinction between my personal and public obligations. I would like to suggest, therefore, that while I cannot deny the justice of your observations regarding the person I would be marrying, I would like to be allowed some time to think over what you have said. Regarding any other matter, I would be most happy to defer to your decision". The king and queen exchanged a glance. If the king was mollified by the placatory answer, he did not show it. On his part, the young man hoped his answer could steer the conversation towards the matter the king had fortuitously brought up. In this, his hopes were not misplaced.

"There is another matter, too, which has been exercising our attention. We have been waiting for your return to announce to the people that you would be heir to the throne. It is, therefore, something that should be done without delay". Though the abrupt announcement dismayed the prince through the imminence of the proposed elevation, he was too relieved at the success of his ploy to divert attention away from the matter of his matrimony, to do anything more than nod his assent. "I shall intimate my minister accordingly and initiate the necessary ceremonies", the king continued, getting up and signifying that the consultations were over.

CHAPTER 17

KING OF VITHALLA

True to his word, within a week the announcement had been made. A period of festivities followed. The priests sat in conclave to determine the most auspicious hour and the exact deities who would have to be propitiated. The people feasted. And on the appointed day, the prince was taken in a ceremonial chariot along a route that had been decorated with festoons for the occasion. The king would have preferred the prince to have traversed the route on a horse, in the traditional manner. But the latter's well known ineptitude as a rider ruled out that method of transport.

Upon the prince's gentle but firm insistence, his younger brother was made to sit with him in the chariot. It was a move that puzzled most people. For, beside the splendid youth of prince Lakkan Pal, the slightly built, dark complexioned figure of the king designate himself was shown to particular disadvantage. If many were puzzled by the move, they would have been astonished if they had known that the contrast—and his own cruel exposure on account of it—was precisely the effect the prince had hoped to achieve. An idea had been taking shape in his mind ever since his meeting with the king. The seed of it had been planted by what he had learned of his younger brother's personality. He had found the latter affable and good natured; and discreet enquiry had elicited the fact that he was popular with the palace staff too. The next step was to talk to him cautiously, to learn the young man's views on such things as governance and the responsibility of rulers towards their subjects.

As he had expected, on these matters he found the young prince had no fixed, or even clear, notions. But what positively delighted him was to find the youngster not unresponsive to the principle that a king had some fundamental obligations to those over whom he ruled. With some surprise, he also discovered that prince Lakkan Pal actually looked up to him; for, it had not occurred to him that the kind of learning he had acquired at Nalanda would have been considered anything more than an esoteric but useless lore. It was then that the fantastic notion had first flashed across his mind. What if the young prince prove malleable enough to be persuaded into accepting that the legitimacy of kingship was conditional upon certain rudimentary obligations to commonweal being met? Could he not be shown a vision that he himself had acquired through a tortuous process that would not have been even initiated but for a teacher like Tara Chand?

It seemed to him then that every available indication pointed to the fact that the younger man would prove to be a much better ruler than himself. That being the case, at the appropriate time why not abdicate in favour of the younger man? 'Make him king', a voice inside him said. 'After that, what is to keep you here and away from Nalanda'. The vision of that return to the university possessed him now. He knew, however, that it was not going to be easy. It could not be in the king's lifetime. And even after that, he would have to make his moves warily. He was realistic enough to realise that there were formidable difficulties. First, prince Lakkan Pal had to be moulded into the kind of sovereign who would wield power with wisdom. Even granting he could achieve this, the abdication would have to find favour with the court and the people. Regarding the former, he was shrewd enough to feel reasonably confident that the move would not be unwelcome. Of the reaction of the people, he was not so sure what it would be. Hence, he resolved that at every opportunity he would propel the younger prince into the public eye—and if it meant that he would suffer from the contrast, that would certainly carry him farther towards his ultimate object. So went his thoughts.

Accordingly, he began to spend some time with his brother every day. He took him out into the city, much as Tara Chand had done with himself. Sometimes they would visit those quarters where the conditions were most wretched. Conscientiously avoiding any attempt at indoctrination, he however matter-of-factly informed the young man how little it took, granted the will, to change those conditions. And, judging from the response he got, he felt he had enough reason to be cautiously optimistic. For, he fancied he saw a dawning appreciation of the situation in the other and even a willingness to address it. He was therefore satisfied with the first part of his strategy.

It was his plan to proceed cautiously to the next stage, since any premature disclosure of his intentions—indeed any suspicion from any quarter—might be fatal to its accomplishment. He had decided that it was essential that the king, especially, should have no inkling of his purpose, at least till it had reached a definite stage. As things turned out, he had no opportunity to find out how well his strategy would have worked. For, a little over a year after he had declared his elder son to be his heir apparent, the old king, after one of the longest reigns in the living memory of his people, passed away. He had been ill only for a few days and the end came swiftly and unexpectedly. But at a little over fifty years of age, he had reached a span of life which was rarely granted to people of that time. Within a few hours after the news of the king's death had been made public, at a hastily convened conclave of a few senior ministers, it was decided that the prince should immediately be installed as the king. The ceremony was perforce an abbreviated one, in view of the pending funeral. The new king conducted his father's obsequies with a ritual thoroughness which not the most conservative priest could cavil at. With the completion of that last duty that he owed his father, he felt his shackles fall from him. The fact of the matter was, that the king had been too remote a figure to his son for the bereavement to cause anything more than a vague sense of loss. In particular, it lacked the poignant edge of that shattering sense of numbing grief that the tidings of his tutor's death had brought. The impassable gulf between their attitudes had further contributed to increasing the distance between them, converting any natural tenderness for a parent to mere filial piety. Accordingly, it was not long before his thoughts turned to the contemplation of the task he had set himself.

He knew however that he had to tread cautiously. The transition from the old rule to the new should be perceived to be a smooth one. Consequently he was in no hurry to inaugurate the new era. But that resolution was shaken when he came to acquaint himself with the affairs of the state and the horrendous mess that had passed for day-to-day governance under his father's rule. There was no record, for instance, of where the taxes came from and where they went. When he set about the task of questioning discreetly the process of revenue collection, the palace official concerned informed him huffily that there had been no necessity to maintain records of it, since, "The king, your majesty's revered father, trusted people more than parchments". It was in the king's mind to respond to the unspoken rebuke with the observation that parchment, after all, had its uses. But, wisely, he forbore.

"Quite so", he replied diplomatically instead, regretting for the first time that he had not had princess Namita as his queen by his side at that instant. He could not help feeling that there was something to be said for the portly princess' methods of handling the perverseness of palace staff. The king realised then that tax revenues were systematically being bled away. But where did they go? Prudently, he decided to go no further into the matter. The general condition of the administration in the other departments was hardly any better and the second realisation stared him in the face that the most pressing need facing him was the establishment of a professionalised civil service to attend to the administration.

But with the state resources haemorrhaging away, he could not wait for the creation of such an institution. In desperation, he now secretly sent word through a messenger to some of his old acquaintances at Nalanda. He needed their help now, he said, in a matter in which he could not trust anybody else. Without mentioning his royal status, he declared that he was now fortunate enough to be in a position to recompense their services in a manner that would exceed their expectations. He was relieved when the messenger returned with the tidings that his erstwhile comrades had agreed to come and had requested a little time to arrange their affairs before embarking upon his. After a six month wait, word finally reached him that a company of them had arrived and were bivouacked just outside the kingdom. The king hurried there forthwith to meet them. It was night when he reached the place and he found a dozen of them gathered around a campfire at the glade. Once greetings had been exchanged, he questioned them avidly about what was happening at the university. However, when he told them that he was now the king of Vithalla, they at first refused to believe him. Scepticism then gave way to amazement, when they realised that their former associate, who had shared a monk's cell with them, was the ruler of a realm.

The king lost no time in acquainting them with the conditions in his kingdom. He required to move immediately on two fronts. First, schools had to be opened to train a corps of young people to serve as the nucleus of a civil service. And till such time as they could be raised to a level when they could be entrusted with administrative responsibilities, he would need a group of his associates to overhaul the administrative system itself—they would be required to create departments, demarcate functions and duties and supervise the building up of a power structure that would allow the king ready access to any information he would want regarding the working of the government. This hugely difficult ask would have to be achieved as unobtrusively as possible; for the king had no illusions about how a hereditary nobility would react when it perceived a threat to the power and privilege it had enjoyed for generations. There was much discussion that followed on these and other matters, before they finally crept into their beds that night. As for the king, as he lay on his back looking up at the glory of the night sky, one thought was uppermost in his mind. He had taken the first step towards his objective. There could be no drawing back, he told himself and resolved that he would go where it led. That was also his last thought before sleep claimed him.

CHAPTER 18

A NOCTURNAL INCIDENT

Though he was a sound sleeper, he slept lightly. Some hours after he had gone to sleep, he woke up. He was not quite sure what it was that had woken him. Possibly a slight sound, he thought, and turned over on his side towards the fire to find it had died down to embers now. By its glow he could see the sleeping figures of the others. It was a moonless night and only the dull glow of the ash covered embers served to illumine the small clearing where they were sleeping. Everything was still; even the small breeze had died down and with it the occasional flutter of the leaves. He was about to go back to sleep, when from the corner of his eye, he caught a small, furtive moment. An inner sense awoke now within him and he could sense that there was danger—deadly danger. And very close. Without opening his eyes further, he tried to see what the movement was that had caught his eye. For the duration of a few long moments there was nothing but the unbroken stillness of the night—a frozen motionlessness so perfect that the scene appeared painted rather than real. Then his eye caught that small movement again. And this time he knew where it was. They were sleeping in the glade and at the edge of it the forest began. This margin was marked by an irregular perimeter of rocks, big and small. The clearing had probably been the work of shepherds who had moved the rocks to the edge to clear a space in the middle. Something near that edge, which he had taken to be a rock by the indistinct light, had moved. He hardly dared to breathe now as he fixed his attention on this strange thing.

There was again a minute or two of absolute stillness. And then the furtive movement. It was surely a living thing—a creature which was either a monkey or a small, misshapen dwarf. The unlikely possibility crossed his mind that it could even be a bear cub. He could not make out anything more by the dim light; nor what manner of creature it was. There was a glint now of something that the creature held. At first the king thought it was a small sword of some sort. But then he decided that it was a long, narrow, cylindrical tube. And it was pointed at him. That sense of danger within him now became an insistent clamour, impelling him to action. His almost overpowering instinct was to leap to his feet, or even shout. But there was a cold, sure knowledge within him that the smallest movement on his part would mean certain death. He willed his body to go limp now and through the slits of his closed eyes, watched the creature. Presently, with an action so swift and so silent that the watching king was hardly aware of it, it had vanished. One moment it had been there crouching and looking at him, and the next, it had melted into the night. He did not know how long he lay there, looking at the vacant spot, before he fell asleep. On getting up in the morning, the first thing he did was to inspect closely the ground where he had seen the creature of the night before. But he found that by design or accident it had been standing at a spot which was hard and rock strewn and gave nothing away. Neither had anybody else seen or heard anything during the night.

Puzzling over this curious incident later on, the king persuaded himself that he must have either dreamed it; or, under the unusual stress of the preceding few days, his brain had started creating phantoms. Anyway, the next few days proved to be crowded with weightier developments that pushed the matter out of his mind. In fact, he would have put it entirely out of his mind, but for a minor, almost trivial, incident that continued to niggle in a corner of it—not that he could even connect it with that night. A few days after this nocturnal conclave had taken place, a delegation of shepherds had come to meet him. Their leader reported to him that over the last few days they had started missing some sheep. Usually, it would be one or two from a flock. On one occasion, late at night, one of the dogs belonging to one of them had started a frenzied barking. The shepherd who had been sleeping some distance away, suspecting an intruder, had hurried to the spot where he had heard the barking. Before he could reach it however, there had proceeded the sounds of a furious scuffle which had suddenly ended in a howl of pain. The dog had started whimpering piteously. On reaching it, he had found it had been badly singed on its neck by what must have been a red hot iron rod or the like.

When the king realised that the spot where all this had happened was not far from the clearing, his interest quickened.

He asked whether the owner of the dog was in the party. A man stepped forward hesitantly. "It is my dog, your majesty", he said.

"Is there anything else you would like to say about this matter?" the king asked him.

The man thought for a few moments, then shook his head slowly. "My dog is brave as a lion your majesty. I have once seen him stand up to a bear without running away. I don't know what kind of man or animal it could have been which had frightened him like that—or inflicted such a grievous wound".

One of the courtiers now stepped forward and sought leave to speak. When the king nodded, he explained that this particular spot was very close to border with the neighbouring kingdom and incidents like these were not unknown in the past. There were incidents when shepherds from either country would help themselves to a few sheep from each other's flocks, he added *sotto voce*. "Your majesty should therefore not give too much thought to this matter", he concluded.

The king looked at him thoughtfully. "What you say may be very well true. But I still cannot understand the injury to the dog. Has anything like that been reported earlier, too?" When the courtier confessed that he could not recall any incident like that, the king now turned to the delegation. "I will see that you are compensated for your loss", he told them. As they were leaving, he called out to the leader. When the man came back, the king told him: "If any other incidents like this happen, I would like them reported personally to me immediately".

CHAPTER 19

THE KING TAKES COUNSEL

As already remarked, in the days that followed the night on the mountain, the initial phase of the plan the king had delineated to the group from Nalanda began to unfold. It was first announced that a deputation of scholars from Nalanda was visiting Vithalla to study the administrative organs and the functioning of government. The king requested the court and its officials to extend any possible assistance the members may require during their stay. Nothing was said about the duration of their visit. For the first week, the members spent their time in moving around the city and the palace. If some of them were seen to be conversing with the people in the streets, nobody attached any particular significance to it. Word had spread that they were former acquaintances of the king and were to be accorded all the hospitality that was traditionally due to a respected guest. Sometime after this, the members of the "Deputation", in twos and threes, went around the various palace rooms which served as offices and where the business of the state was being conducted.

They seemed to be paying diligent heed to the proceedings and were seen to be taking notes. The majority of the officials were, on the whole, pleased by the attention they were getting and willingly answered any questions that were put to them. The "learning" went on apace. So much so, before long, it was not uncommon to see some of the members "helping" out the clerks, by doing the more routine parts of their work. And, inevitably, this involvement grew. From the point of view of the officials, they could see no reason to decline what they looked upon as unpaid help. On their part, the 'scholars' were scrupulous not to press their help or involvement, in those rare instances when they sensed any reluctance from any palace official to such an offer.

After this had been going on for some time, there was a confidential meeting with the members of the delegation in the king's chambers. "You must have been able to form some opinion by this time of the state of affairs" began the king.

Tham, the youngest among them, stood up now. "If Your Majesty will permit me . . . .", he began. The king motioned him to his seat. "My Majesty will certainly permit you, Tham. As a matter of fact, it can't wait to hear you out". He regarded them for a long moment. "Let me make something plain to you all, if I haven't already done so. We're gathered here as equals and it is I who am indebted to you all. I am Ram Pal of Nalanda, inside this room. In fact, since the chief object of this entire exercise is to restore me to that state, all this exalted address and the other tokens of reverence we shall reserve for the court, where it is necessary to keep up certain appearances a bit longer. We haven't time enough for all those silly ceremonials here. Will you tell me now, Tham, what it is you wanted to say?"

The young man paused to collect his thoughts. "Things appear to be very bad here", he said finally. "I've been looking at the administration of justice, for instance. Do you know that it's impossible for the poor to get anything decided in their favour?"

"Can you give me an example?"

A wry smile broke on the young man's face. "More than you can want", he said. "There was a case recently of a nobleman who had to celebrate his son's wedding. He told the serfs on his land that they had to raise a certain sum of money by a certain time. It was plain extortion. You see, it was beyond their ability to raise a tenth of the amount. They had already been beggared by what they were paying as rent",

"And then . . . ."

"When they couldn't meet the demand, the peasants were thrashed. The grain they had stored as seed for the next sowing season was taken away, their houses burnt down. They were finally dispossessed of the land too".

"Then they approached the court?"

"They did. And were told that there could be no question of redress for an act that had the sanction of the king".

The king who had been listening to this recital with expressionless attention, sat up bolt upright now. "What did you say?" he asked.

The young man shrugged. "You see, according to the judge, he was presented with an order which had your signature on it. What he meant was that it had the royal seal on it. Which in turn meant that the nobleman in question had a gold piece to buy the right to affix it on the order and the necessary connections needed to access such a service". Tham stopped and looked at the king. "This is the kind of thing that goes on routinely here. You must first put an end to this systematic abuse of your authority, Ram Pal. Otherwise your people are going to think that every act of tyranny perpetrated here—and there are plenty—has your personal sanction. As I see it, therefore, you need to embark upon two kinds of corrective measures. The first is relatively easy and can be done tomorrow. You must entrust the royal seal to some trustworthy court official and make it clear to him that it will be his responsibility to ensure that it is not abused. So that, barring a few routine matters, whenever the official is required to use the seal, he should get it personally cleared by you. What the situation demands is accountability. That will go a long way towards remedying this problem".

The king looked wonderingly at the slight figure of the youth. He was human enough to feel a stab of envy, that in the time it had taken him to come to grips with the problem, the other had already penetrated to its solution. "I shall attend to that immediately", he said. "Now tell me about your second measure".

"Actually, I had discussed that with Sanathan", said Tham. He turned towards another member of the group.

"Can you explain it?" he asked. If the king had been impressed with Tham's clear-sightedness, he was even more agreeably struck by the deft diplomacy with which the young man involved everybody in the discussion and thereby deflected an undue amount of attention from himself. The person thus invited to speak, cleared his throat.

"The second phase of your campaign is certainly more difficult. You will have to draw up two lists—one, of people who will support you in your attempt to reform the administration and the other from whom you can expect opposition. You can trust on a few powerful allies, fortunately. Among them, most importantly, is your General. And the morale of the army is also reasonably high".

It was Tham who spoke again now. "But you are also going to have influential and powerful enemies. Unfortunately, a majority of those who are powerful now are those who stand to lose the most in your reform process. And they are not going to allow themselves to be marginalised without putting up a fight". Tham paused to look at another member of the party. "This is where your strategy becomes important, Som".

The person addressed was a senior member of the group. "You see, Ram Pal", he began, "From what you've heard, it must be clear to you that by the time your intention to reform the institutions of governance becomes evident, you are going to need supporters. So I suggest that you unobtrusively start forming an inner cabal of close confidants even now. Again, I think that your General—Verma isn't it?" the speaker paused to look at Sanathan, who nodded. "I believe Verma should be among them. You must show him you trust him. In fact, you should go farther and start consulting him on affairs of the state".

In the days that followed, as the king turned these recommendations over in his mind, the obvious force of the arguments began to get more apparent. Once a course of action had been identified and discussed, it seemed to him that the situation was not one that offered any other alternative. He had also decided that the time had come to take the prince into his confidence. It would not be necessary to tell him yet about the abdication. But prince Lakkan Pal should know about what was happening and why a delegation of scholars from a far-off university should have suddenly got interested in the governance of his country.

CHAPTER 20

"... SOMEBODY ...
OR SOMETHING ... INSIDE"

It had become something of a habit with the king to go up to the little glade and spend some time with himself whenever he had something on his mind that he wished to think through. He would ask to be taken halfway up the hill on the chariot and then walk up the rest of the way on a steep footpath that wound up to it. Quite often day would be breaking by the time he returned. This time he took the young prince with him. It seemed to him that for the kind of communication he wished to make, the glade would be a better place than the palace, with its manifold distractions.

It was a dark night as the brothers trudged uphill on the narrow footpath. The king started talking slowly about the condition of the country when their father had died and he himself had taken over—the wretchedness of the people, the appalling state of the administrative machinery and the things he had talked over with old Tara Chand. He came finally to the things that he had decided had to be done. The prince who had been listening intently, looked at him. "And so it was that you brought these people—your former friends—here, to assist you in this matter?"

"Yes", said the king, after a pause. "Not merely to assist me, but . . . ." The king broke off now as he realized that his companion's attention was somewhere else. The latter was standing still, staring at something some distance away to his right. When the king turned to see what it was, he could just make out something burning in the distance. "It must be some shepherd's fire, Lakki", said the king. They wander all over the place here. I have seen . . ."

"No *Bhaiyya*. That is no shepherd's fire. There is something very strange going on there. I thought I saw some children running towards it".

"Children?", asked the king, startled. There was a memory stirring within him now. He saw in his mind's eye the apparition he had seen on the night he had slept in the clearing. "Come", he said. "Let's find out what it is". Progress through the heavy underbrush was not easy. At times they had to stop and hack their way through with their swords. As they neared the fire, the king realised what the younger man had meant. Their descending course would have taken them a few feet below the glade and a few hundred steps from it. As they approached it they could see the fire raging at close quarters. The object that was on fire appeared to them like a large, smooth, shiny egg. It could have accommodated three men inside it, thought the king. But the strangest thing about it was the fire itself. The huge, rounded shape seemed to be hissing and spitting long thin serpent tongues of multicoloured flame—green and gold and red and purple. They danced like streamers on an unfelt wind. It seemed to be sorcery, to the astonished pair; so unlike it was to anything they had ever experienced. As they stood there gazing awestruck at the spectacle, a thin, whistling cry came from the egg. The king was the first to come out of the stupor the scene had induced in them.

"There's somebody inside it Lakki", he said. And then added almost to himself ; "Or something". He turned to the younger man now. "Quick. We must put out the fire. Otherwise, whoever is inside is going to get roasted". The prince joined him now and they began to throw handfuls of earth at the burning egg. But they might have as well saved themselves the trouble, for the fire raged without any sign of lessening. The heat and the smoke by this time was becoming unbearable. The king paused in his labours to look at the conflagration in desperation. He plucked some bushes from the ground and as much green foliage as he could gather and threw them on the fire—with no more effect than the first method had produced. "It's no use", said the prince. "We can do nothing". As they stood back from the fire with soot blackened faces and singed clothes, looking at the weird alchemy of the fire, the prince suddenly stiffened and gripped his brother's hand. "*Bhaiyya*. Look there". The words came out in a whisper.

He was staring intently at a spot a few feet from where they stood. At first the king could make out nothing through the through the thick swirling smoke that suffocated him and stung his eyes. Then he saw it. There was a large tree and at the foot of it something seemed to be sitting on the ground. It appeared to be a creature about the size of a year old calf, with bright protruding eyes. Sensing that it had been seen, the creature tried to move. They saw then that between the two upper limbs and the feet like appendages on which it seemed to be standing erect, there was a thin flap of skin which gave it the appearance of a bat's wing. Imagine, if you can, a huge bat, four feet high and walking awkwardly. As they stood petrified, the king realized that what he had seen that night in the glade had neither been a dream nor the product of an overheated imagination.

Suddenly another whistling scream issued from the egg. The king could see now that a small hatch was partially open at the top. But the flames around it would have scorched anybody who had tried to climb out through it. As they stood there watching helplessly, the creature at the edge of the clearing now advanced towards them with short waddling steps. The prince's hand flew instinctively to the hilt of his sword. The weapon flashed out and in an instant would have lunged in a fatal thrust when the king's voice rang out: "Wait". The word was spoken with an authority which prince Lakkan Pal had never heard from his elder brother. His arm was frozen in mid movement. The creature's ungainly progress stopped when it was a few feet from them and a strange medley of sounds—gurgles, squeaks and whistles—issued from it. It seemed to be looking at them intently. Suddenly the king gasped. It was as if a series of visions had risen in his mind—a confused jumble of scenes and pictures of which he could not say whether they were actually happening before him or whether some strange trick of memory were presenting to him.

A persistent image now arose. It was of a creature like the one that stood before him. Only, this one was inside the egg. It was breathing laboriously with rasping gasps and life was clearly ebbing out of it. The stream of images ceased as suddenly it had begun. As the creature stood there looking at him, the king saw in its eyes an expression he could not read. It seemed to him that there was an imploring entreaty in it. Suddenly a thought flashed through his mind, of something he had once seen and forgotten in the course of one of his rambles in that region.

"Lakki", he said, "there is one chance. Come with me quickly. There is no time to lose". With that he began to clamber up the hillside like a madman, slashing with his sword through the matted and tangled undergrowth, oblivious of the thorn bushes and the tree branches that scratched and whipped him. The younger man was by his side in a moment. "*Bhaiyya,* what . . . .".

"No", said the king urgently, without pausing in his labours. "Not now. I'll tell you later". A few minutes later they found themselves at a point almost directly above the fire. But the king's attention was on something else now. They were now standing at the edge of a large pool of water. Most of it lay in the interior of a natural grotto. The pool was fed by a slow ooze from a fissure in the rock wall at the back. The overflow from it had formed a natural rivulet in the rainy season that ran through the spot where the inferno was now raging. Under the dark night sky, the pool lay like a black mirror. Along the outer edge of it, stood two or three huge boulders. The king now ran to the largest of these and started to heave at it. And then the watching prince understood his brother's purpose. In three bounds he joined the latter and bracing his feet on the earth, applied his own muscle upholstered shoulder to the rock. The boulder which had hardly budged under the king's efforts now began to shake and shudder. The corded sinews of the young man's shoulder and back now leapt out into ridges and valleys of tremendous power, while the veins along his neck and arms stood out like ropes under the terrific strain. For a moment, nothing seemed to happen. The rock seemed to be too deeply imbedded in the earth. However, under the unremitting application of that tremendous force, slowly but surely, the rock was giving way. It began to lean out more and more, till the soil, softened by water seepage could no longer hold it. It suddenly gave way now and tilted away from the pool, without quite falling down. But that was enough. Through the space where the rock had been, a torrent of water now rushed out and a frothing flood poured down the rivulet and washed irresistibly over the burning orb.

There was an angry hiss and clouds of vapour rose, obscuring everything for a moment. But under that deluge the fire did not stand a chance. It died with a sputter and finally the steam clouds too ceased. The cascading water, too, had largely lessened in volume as the water level had fallen in the reservoir above, by the time the two of them returned to the scene. As they stood looking at the strange object that had been afire, the hatch on the top slowly opened. The creature that came out of it was another of the kind they had seen earlier. It was clearly exhausted and on emerging, fell out of the egg shaped contrivance into the puddle of hot water that had formed; then it got up and slowly began to drag itself away. The king walked up to the shell now and gingerly placed his hands on it. It was smooth and hot to the touch, with wisps of steam issuing from it still. It was presumably some sort of metal, he decided, though none that he had seen before. With the prince helping him, he ascended the earthen wall behind it and tried to peer into the hatch. However, he found that it was too small to allow him an entry and it was too dark to see anything inside.

By the time the king had clambered down and looked for the creatures, there was no evidence of any of them; they had apparently taken advantage of their benefactors' preoccupation to return to whatever hiding place they had made for themselves. The king then turned his attention to his companion. Tenderly he bathed and cleansed the lacerations where the rock had scored and gashed the mighty arch of the young prince's muscle corded back. Then, after some time spent in looking around, they decided that it would serve no purpose to stay there any longer The king decided that the next day he would have the shell transported back to the city.

CHAPTER 21

THE KING ADVANCES A THEORY

They walked back slowly along the way they had come, in silence, till the king broke it. "Are you worried, Lakki?", he asked.

The young man did not answer immediately. "I think so", he replied finally. "Maybe a little frightened too, by what we saw". The king looked at him quickly.

"I think I know enough about you to say that you are as fearless as any man can be. But it is when we encounter something that lies completely beyond our experience . . . ." They walked farther in silence.

"I've heard of some very odd creatures which live beyond the Northern mountains, *bhaiyya*. These must have come from there. Did you see how the creature came out of the burning egg?" Getting no response from the king, the prince decided that the question had not penetrated the other's pre-occupation. But when he spoke, finally, it was in reply to the query.

"These are not creatures from there, Lakki", he said slowly. "In fact, I doubt we will ever find out where they came from. And that shell was not an egg, though it looked like one".

"What is it then?"

The king smiled. "I didn't say I knew what it is". After a moment he added. "But I can tell you what I *think* it is". The prince looked at him questioningly. "I think it's something the creatures use to travel in, like the way we use a chariot". The prince regarded him with perplexity. "But . . . but . . . , there were no wheels . . . no horses . . . What are you saying?"

The king was gazing into the far distance with frowning concentration. "There are a lot of things I don't know about this, Lakki. Remember I am only advancing some surmises—in other words, guessing most of the things I'm going to talk about". The prince waited patiently.

"Suppose you wanted to be taken to the glade on your chariot. Would that have been possible?"

The prince shook his head. "Because a chariot requires a path to drive over; and there isn't one that goes up to the top of the hill".

They had been walking along slowly as they had been speaking. The king stopped now to look at the clear night sky. After he had stood contemplating it in absorbed concentration for a minute or two, he raised his arm to point at it. "Suppose now that you wanted to reach one of those stars, of what use would a chariot or wheels or horses be to you?"

"I agree it would be completely useless. But . . . ." He stopped as the meaning of what the other was saying suddenly sank in. "You mean . . . ." His eyes widened as he looked at his brother. The king was not sure whether the expression on it was one of horror or astonishment.

He placed an arm about the younger man's shoulders. "Remember my warning that I'm talking about things I know nothing about. If you promise to hold fast to this understanding, and all that it implies, I shall continue". The prince looked at his elder brother and nodded uncertainly.

"As I was saying, supposing you wanted to reach a star from here, or even the moon, all the normal methods of travelling over land would be useless. We cannot have an adequate idea of what one would need to travel over those colossal voids. Now I am going to put two unununderstandable facts to reach what appears even to me as an even more unrealistic conclusion. Would it be possible, I ask myself, whether these creatures that we saw are from another world and that the egg shaped object was some kind of vehicle—possibly one of those they have been using for many years for their transport in reaching this place". The younger man looked at him.

"I have often wondered what it was that drew you to such a faraway place like Nalanda and kept you there for so many years. I see now the value of the learning you have acquired there", he said humbly.

The king looked at him quickly, then shook his head. "Learning, of course, has many advantages, Lakki", he said. "But it was not my learning that makes me guess where these creatures come from. You see, a fortunate accident delivered into my hands a vital key that led to that understanding. It was taken to be a toy made of gold. But I will tell you more about what it is, one day". They stood there quietly for a moment, then, before the king took the younger man's hand in his. "Come", he said, "It's already late".

After they proceeded a few steps, he started talking again. "That would also explain the fire. I've heard at Nalanda that fire is a way of transforming and getting energy, Lakki. I suspect that something must have happened and they had lost control just before they came down". They did not speak much the rest of the way, each of them busy with his own thoughts, till they reached the city.

"When we get that shell to the city tomorrow, you will be able to find out what is, won't you *bhaiyya*?" the prince asked then.

The king looked at him thoughtfully. "You have too much faith in my powers, Lakki", he said. Then he shook his head. "But I'll tell you something. That shell, or egg, or whatever it is—I have a feeling we won't see it again".

CHAPTER 22

THE WARLORD

In this prophecy the king was to be proved wrong. But when the men who had been sent to carry the shell to the city the next day reached the spot, they found not a trace of it there. All the evidence was there, of course, of the events of the previous night—the spot itself, charred and burnt by the fire, the course the water had taken and on the pool above, the great rock fallen on the ground now, like an overthrown foeman. But of the huge egg-like shell the men could find no trace. Nor did report reach them of anything unusual happening in that locality—so that, had it not been for the undeniable evidence of that adventure they would almost have dismissed it as a figment of the imagination, much as the king himself had done earlier with what he had seen at night in the glade. One question, however, persisted with its nagging presence: what could be the purpose of the creatures' presence?

But, as on the earlier occasion, there were developments that turned their minds away from speculations in that direction. Only, this time, they were more serious. At that time, to the North East lay the kingdom of Kanija, with its capital at Mahimapur. It was ruled by king Vichint, who claimed descent from Bhim, the mythical hero of the epic *Mahabharat*. Upon accession to the throne, his first act was to rechristen Mahimapur as Bhimpur and the second, to start gathering a large army. When tidings of Vichint's activities reached king Ram Pal of Vithalla, he began to wonder what was coming next; for, Vichint had already begun to acquire a reputation for an ungovernably vicious temper and a capacity for unprovoked violence which went with that trait.

One of the stories about him, for instance, concerned an occasion when he was drinking with his wife's two brothers inside the fort that enclosed a part of the royal palace. One of the courtiers narrated to the two princes how he had seen the king run around the sentry platform that went around the fort wall on the inside, with a man under either arm. The audience had had the misfortune to smile at the story. Whereupon, Vichint had stood up wordlessly and picked them up, one under each arm like a pair of children. The king was a giant in stature, like his mythical and heroic forbear and was half a head taller than the next tallest man in the region. He then calmly climbed up the ladder to the platform, with the two young men smiling to cover their alarm at what they perceived to be a joke being carried too far. The king had then run around the platform. Upon completing the circuit, he had looked at the cheering throng below and then, to their horror, hurled the young men down.

There were other stories, too, about the megalomaniac king of Kanija—his prodigious strength and his dissoluteness. The king of Vithalla was not sure how many of these to believe, or how many had even a grounding in fact. In any case, there were things more pressing to occupy him than the antics of Kanij's impetuous king. But when intelligence reached him that the maniacal monarch was marching with a mighty host of over twenty thousand men in a direction which would bring him to the gates of Vithalla in a month, he was suddenly obliged to consider Vichint's motives with a seriousness which he could not have thought possible ere that. He took counsel then, first with his ministers and nobles and then with his companions from Nalanda. Not that he could find a shred of comfort from any quarter.

The fact was that the region was a chequerboard of little kingdoms, principalities and potentates that had long ago realised the futility of waging war to gain any substantial end. The distribution of material resources was more or less equitable among them and none had much to gain by the acquisition of territory—assuming that it would be possible to hold on to such gains for any length of time. There was also a homogeneity of culture and custom that precluded any perception of alienation which, in turn, could have led to strife. What conflicts there were, were therefore of an internecine or civil nature, fuelled usually by sibling rivalry.

Unschooled, therefore, in martial arts and too exhausted by the conditions under which they lived to be roused to valiant defence by a call to arms against an overwhelmingly stronger aggressor, it was a largely peaceable community that the warlord of Kanija encountered when he sallied forth with irresistible force. Kingdom after kingdom capitulated in a series of short but bloody and brutal encounters. From what inevitably followed these conquests, it was apparent that it was not so much a war of conquest and annexation that Vichint had in mind as a campaign of pillage and loot. And he left a trail of smoking ruin behind him, as the grim markers of his march.

As soon as word had reached Vithalla, the preparations for the defence of the kingdom had begun in earnest. From the foaming flood of the Vajravallabha, the river that by an informal understanding marked the Eastern boundary of the kingdom, a concealed canal was now dug that carried water inside the fort. Earthen ramparts had hastily been constructed at points where the natural defences were perceived to be weakest. And at other vulnerable points deep trenches were dug and the water from the canal were led into these, turning their bottom into a morass of mire and water, thereby converting them into an improvised but effective moat. The floor of these were now planted with sharpened stakes. New granaries were built and food stocks that would last a few months at least were stored. And, finally, of the three bridges over the Vajravallabha, two were cut down and only the largest of the three remained. Through this, a daily stream of people from neighbouring kingdoms and their livestock and wagons, carrying all variety of goods from grains and vegetables to household goods, poured into the city every day, seeking desperate sanctuary.

A murmur rose now and ran around at all these preparations. Was not the king surely neglecting his primary duty to strengthen the army, in the midst of preparing for a siege? The truth of the matter was that few knew the views that had been presented in the council of war that had been held prior to the decision to make all these preparations. If they had, they would have had even more reason to be worried. For, it had clearly shown the futility of opposing Vichint's marauding host. The council had begun with speaker after speaker urging the immediate necessity of conscripting every able bodied young man into the army and preparing them under a severely rigorous regime of militaristic training for the stern task ahead. Indeed, there was a school of opinion that held that the army should be augmented by a mercenary force.

Vithalla's men would not flinch from facing death, declared a senior minister. Vichint would know what it was to stalk a sheep into a cave and find it to be a lion's den, said another. The hall resounded to the rafters with affirmations of patriotic resolve. Through all this discussion, the king had listened with an expressionless mien and had spoken almost nothing. At the end of these ringingly heroic affirmations, the king turned to Vikram Verma, the General of Vithalla's army. "There are certain matters on which I would require clarification from you, General", he began. Verma stood up and bowed. "First I would like to know what the strength of our forces is—that is, if we need to press them into service in the next few days, say".

The answer came after a moment's hesitation. "Between seventeen hundred to eighteen hundred, sire".

The king now addressed the assembly. "Does anyone know what the strength of king Vichint's army is?" A medley of voices arose, offering estimates varying from six thousand to twelve thousand. "Very good", said the king. "I think we can say that your guess would be ten thousand at a median estimate". There was silence now as they waited for what he was going to say.

The king unrolled a parchment-like scroll and consulted it. "When Vichint set out from Kanij, the size of his expeditionary force was around twenty thousand. Nobody had any more accurate estimate of it. I doubt whether Vichint himself knew. I suspect that he is not the sort of person who allows himself to be bothered by logistics and figures. His strength is action and not strategy". The king looked around before continuing. "He had passed through six kingdoms and looted them comprehensively, when the messengers last brought me the news. Of those, the remnants of the armies of the first three kingdoms—that is, the soldiers who had survived the slaughter—have *joined* his expeditionary force, attracted by the prospect of plunder". The king looked up again from the parchment at the assembly. There was dead silence now. "The number of these come to around three thousand from each kingdom, roughly. As I've already said, nobody has an idea of what the actual numbers are. I would therefore say that we are facing *an army of thirty thousand soldiers.* And against this we can muster eighteen hundred men—men who are basically little more than so many peasants, many of them armed with staves, mattocks and scythes". He paused. "If there is any disagreement with any fact I have presented, I would invite it now". There was another silence. "What would your majesty suggest?", asked Verma hesitantly.

"I'll come to that soon. I want to say something before that. I have been thinking for some time now that what the little kingdoms in this valley need is a confederacy that can defend itself against such external aggressors. But that measure itself must follow a pact of peace and common defence between us. All that, of course, lies in the future. But maybe Vichint has already done us a good turn. This crisis may be just what we need for such a confederacy to take shape. In fact, when he started his campaign, I dispatched messengers to the other kingdoms to sound them out on the possibility of coming together". The king shook his head slowly. "For the present there is not much choice before us except shoring up our defence fortifications. I have a few concrete proposals to make and I would like your views and suggestions on these".

What these proposals were and the measures they resulted in, has already been seen. That these proposals did not meet with general approval, has also been remarked. When this was reported to the king, he received the news with his customary thoughtfulness. "I can understand that unease", he said. "In fact, I share it myself. I only hope I haven't made a terrible mistake. I think we are going to find out soon enough", he said. The dawn of the third day after this observation was made, showed how right he had been. For, when the sun rose on that day, it was to reveal on the farther bank of the river a sight to fill the stoutest heart in Vithalla with dread. On the Eastern bank of the Vajravallabha stood the massed forces of the invaders, with the giant figure of their dread chieftain in plain view at the head of it. Rank upon rank the host extended, beyond reach of the eye. And it was also clear now why they stood there without advancing any further. Two huge piers supported the bridge on the farther side; and from either of these, a formidable chain led to the other end. It was clear that at the first attempt to cross the bridge, the chains would be pulled and the piers and the bridge they supported would collapse into the river.

CHAPTER 23

"AN ACT OF COWARDICE"

As soon as news had reached the palace, the king had convened his council. A discussion was in progress now—it was a fierce debate that raged. The consensus was that the bridge should immediately be pulled down to deny the invaders entry to the city. As usual, after he had patiently heard everybody out, the king himself was the last to speak. "Thirty miles to the north the river broadens out and there it can be easily forded. At almost the same distance to the south, there is another ford. We have strengthened our fortifications at these points to the extent our slender resources allow. Forty miles to the south, in the kingdom of Vaisala, there are two bridges. So, by bringing the bridge down, we can buy ourselves another day, maybe. What happens after that? When I started strengthening the walls and ramparts, I had hoped not to hold out for months against Vichint, but to create the impression that we could". He paused.

"We have an adversary who does not have a shred of patience. If he cannot capture a city in a matter of days and sack it, he loses patience. It's impossible for him to play a waiting game. And that is exactly what I wish to tell him when I meet him". In the silence that followed this matter-of-fact announcement, nobody dared to speak. Prince Lakkan Pal it was who finally broke the silence. "Are you . . . Do you . . . Are you saying that you intend to meet this man?" The king looked at his younger brother. "I am, Lakki. I am going to make him an offer. My strategy is built around the fact that it will be presented to him in a way that he will find it difficult to refuse". He stopped. "In convening this council, it was my primary objective to discuss this with you".

"I'm going to request all of you gathered here to grant me the indulgence of first patiently listening to me before you start expressing your opinion and then be completely honest in doing it. Indeed, we have little time to observe convoluted courtesies of court procedure. I have no wish to waste any more time and shall apprise you of my plan in the fewest words possible. It is, that remembering that with Vichint we are dealing not so much with a man as a monster bent upon rapine and plunder rather than conquest, I suggest we give it to him ourselves. I hope that from everything we have already discussed, it would have become clear that with an army the size of his, it would be futile for us to try to resist him indefinitely. He is ultimately going to take what he wants from us, in spite of any resistance from us that would be as valiant as it would be doomed. We shall lose thousands of our people and this city would be fed to fire.

Bearing this in mind, what I propose doing is to go to him with an offer. I am going to tell him that he will be allowed to enter the city with twenty five hundred chosen men. They will be treated as the guests of this kingdom. They will spend three days here. During that time they can make a hoard of anything that they can and want to carry away. On the third day they will be allowed to leave the city with whatever booty they have collected, on condition they would leave us in peace".

There was a stunned silence when the king stopped speaking. It was prince Lakkan Pal again, who was the first to recover from his shock. He leapt to his feet. "It is not an act that befits a king, *bhaiyya*. It is an act of cowardice that betrays the people of this country". The prince's face was flushed. As he stood in his place, he was trembling with the fury that had mastered him.

"Remember whom you are speaking to, my prince". It was Verma who had interjected now, as he stood up and faced the young man. The king got up at that, walked quickly to his general and spoke quietly to him. The older man sat down slowly, without taking his eyes off the younger man. When the king returned to his seat, he turned to look at the prince. "Sit down, Lakki and be patient with me. I'll answer your charge. But first I must express my appreciation of your honesty in expressing yourself without reserve. You have talked about betraying the people. Is it your argument then, that in order to stand by the people of this country, I shall have to allow thousands of men to be slaughtered or taken into slavery—that it would be immoral to 'buy' peace with the plunder that Vichint is going to take anyway?" The king broke off to look at the assembly. "If that is so, then I prefer that immorality to the honour of the other course".

In the silence that followed, one of the senior ministers stood up. "Does your majesty have reason to believe Vichint will accept your offer?"

"I don't have reason to believe anything", was the king's reply. "But I'm hoping that if I am successful in my attempt to intimate to Vichint that we are prepared for an extended siege, the prospect may just prompt him to accept my offer". The king paused before continuing. "I would finally urge upon those gathered here the necessity to ask yourself how many of our people would choose a gloriously futile death, defending the indefensible, rather than contribute their share to a tribute, if by doing so, not only they, but their children, would be allowed to live".

It was a chastened prince Lakkan Pal who stood up now. "I spoke like a fool, *bhaiyya*. Forgive me. But will you permit me to offer one last alternative?"

"I'll be very happy to listen to anything you want to say, Lakki. The point of convening this assembly is give everybody an opportunity to express his opinion". Whatever it was on the prince's mind must have been a weighty matter; for even with this encouragement, he seemed to be finding it difficult to find the right words. "It seems to me that there is a more . . . forgive me for saying this, but there is a more honourable way out of this". He stopped now to look at the king in some confusion.

"Tell me", said the king. "What is this way?"

"*Bhaiyya*, I see why you want to avoid war at all cost. But suppose I challenge Vichint to a personal combat?"

It was the king's turn to be astonished. "Personal combat?" he echoed. He took his time to consider, then said musingly: "Such things aren't unknown. I suppose one of us could challenge him", he said after a pause. "If I challenge him, he will accept it immediately and slay me before my sword clears my scabbard. But you . . . .", the king's voice trailed off into silence now.

"I stand more than a chance against him, *bhaiyya*", he said eagerly. There was a hot flush on the young man's face now. "I'll face him with a sword, while I have heard that he fights with a huge battle axe. Let us see who wins".

The king smiled. "I've also heard that he wields that axe with as much effort as a cowherd carrying a flute". He looked at the splendid figure of the young man standing before him, then shook his head slowly. "If he accepts, it'll be a bear taking on a panther. He may be a monster, but he's not a fool, Lakki. He knows that there will be a risk and he'll laugh your challenge off. On the other hand", said the king, speaking slowly, "if he accepts and something should happen to you, I cannot face our mother after that. No, no Lakki, it is a valiant offer, but it cannot be considered". It was late afternoon by the time the discussion wound to its inevitable and weary end. As the king had known, the discussion only served to reveal the fact that there was no reasonable alternative to his proposal.

It was further decided that early next morning the king would personally convey this message to the man who commanded the predatory army that stood waiting outside Vithalla's gates. The king had also insisted that it should be he who should bear the message. His reason had been that the most crucial part of the mission would be the negotiation that should logically follow the offer, and none but he should be entrusted with the task. He had, however, another unstated private reason. He had no illusions about the personal danger to anybody who would go to parley with a madman like the warlord of Kanija and he believed that he himself would run a lesser risk than a minister, in that role. In spite of the considerable unease of all those present, the king finally had his way.

CHAPTER 24

THE TRAP

The shadows were lengthening that day when a messenger went to the bridge. He walked three quarters of it. At that point he was met by a man from the other side to whom he communicated the information that the next day the king of Vithalla would meet King Vichint with a proposal. There was a bellow from the giant when the message reached him. He grabbed a spear from a soldier, strode up to the end of the bridge and hurled it towards the other end. The spear arced through the air, cleared the bridge and landed on the earth on the farther side. "Come out and fight you cowards. You cannot hide forever from me", he thundered. If any man in Vithalla had an answer to that invitation, it was struck from him by this demonstration of the terrific strength of the Colossus that commanded the troops on the farther side. For, every man who watched it knew the prodigious power of arm it would have taken to throw that spear to half the length of the bridge. There would be few indeed, in Vithalla, who would have been capable of even such a feat.

There was a brief meeting that night between Vichint and half a dozen of his trusted lieutenants in the king's tent. If there was one man in the world who dared to counsel him, it was the elderly councillor of state, Kishan Dev. But the wily old councilor also knew exactly how much he could rein in his sovereign's tempestuous instincts and as a concession to the latter's impatience had given in to Vichint's insistence that they should launch forthwith into action, rather than wait to see what terms Vithalla's king would offer the next day. Accordingly, it was decided that a hand-picked expeditionary force of two thousand men would cross the river at the ford to the North, enter the city, hack through whatever resistance there was and gain control of the bridge by morning. While it was not the sort of strike that Kishan Dev would himself have favoured, he had to grant that the plan stood more than a reasonable chance of succeeding.

Accordingly, under cover of the darkness, the troop crossed the ford. Though they did not know it till hours later, that was when things began to go disastrously wrong for them. For, precisely in anticipation of such a contingency, Vithalla's king had posted sentries there, as also at the second ford to the south. So that, even before the men had finished the crossing, the defenders had made their deadly preparations. Dawn had begun to streak the sky by the time Vichint's men had finished what they believed to be their stealthy crossing. They massed together on the opposite bank and quietly stole up to the ramparts. These were completely unscaleable. But on moving a bit farther along the earthen wall, they came to a place where there was a break in the rampart which ran for a couple of hundred yards. They had no right to know that by this time, their every move was being observed and reported to the troops guarding that section of the wall, by a system of yanks and pulls on sections of rope, corresponding to a pre-assigned code. The ruler of Vithalla was proving himself to be an unlikely military genius.

The invaders were marching in a roughly rectangular phalanx and had advanced two hundred yards into the interior when a sentry 'dozing' around a small fire, a hundred yards ahead, 'suddenly' noticed them and gave the alarm. As he fled now, the expeditionary force saw a group of dozen or so soldiers, who had apparently been sleeping on the farther side of a long, low mound, now scramble to their feet and start looking around for their weapons. That piece of amateur theatricals had been pretty well rehearsed. Abandoning any further attempt at concealment, Vichint's men now raced towards their quarry with blood curdling whoops. At this, the little group of defenders seemed to be caught in paralysed indecision whether to stand their ground and be slaughtered or to flee. Finally they seemed to decide on the first strategy and advanced towards the intruders. But after taking ten steps they stopped and looked uncertainly at the swiftly advancing foe. A shrewder commander would have realized that there was something extremely odd about this behaviour. But the man who was at the head of that two thousand strong contingent was one who had been chosen for his proven fearlessness in battle, rather than for any conspicuous distinction in the tactics of warfare. Indeed, his redoubtable chieftain could himself hardly be less disdainful about what he considered to be a lot of bookish rubbish. And to be fair, the size of Vichint's army had made all theories of military manoeuvre irrelevant. But fearlessness, unfortunately, has rarely been known to contribute significantly to longevity.

When the leaders of that headlong rush were hardly fifty feet away from the petrified little band of ten people, they suddenly felt the solid ground under their feet give way and with a horrified scream hundreds of men fell now into the cunningly hidden moats, where they died a horrible death. And their leader, proving he had come by his reputation for intrepidity deservedly, was among the first to perish. The men behind clambered over the bodies of their comrades, uncertain about what had happened, in the semi-light. They regrouped now, a chastened lot and continued their movement in the general direction of advance. There was enough light by now to see the low earthen mound that stood a hundred yards away. The march was resumed now and they would have moved half way towards the mound when terror struck for the second time. The advancing line was barely fifty yards away when 'the mound' seemed suddenly to rise before the marching column. The invaders found themselves facing a line of two hundred archers who had been concealed under a thick cloth on which grass had been strewn. Before the astonished men, leaderless and demoralised, could even turn around, the bows began to sing. Death rained on the fleeing men as the arrows began to fly thick and fast as deadly raindrops. They turned back now and fled from warfare of a kind they had never encountered till then, nor had even heard of, all thoughts of advance finally abandoned; back they went again, clambering over the moats of death. But a further doom now awaited the decimated fliers. They found their exit blocked. There now stood another line of archers in the breach in the ramparts through which they had entered. Arrows began to hum again and fly like hornets of death, sowing doom where they fell and stung. In that hellish hail, hundreds perished as volley after volley of withering fusillades was poured into the hapless host. When the remainder finally threw down their weapons and cried for mercy, less than half the number that had entered was taken prisoner. More than a thousand of Vichint's fiercest fighters had fallen in the deadly ambush.

CHAPTER 25

Two Kings

It was morning by the time the tidings reached the king of Vithalla. He received the news gravely. "Vichint has forced my hand", he said thoughtfully. "I'll have to act fast now". Upon the king's suggestion, it was decided that the news of the disastrous nocturnal campaign launched by Vichint was to be kept secret for the present. "For, once that information reaches him, my life would not be worth an hour's purchase", declared the king. With that, he ordered a chariot to be ready.

The prince spoke up now. "You have turned down my request to challenge Vichint to a personal combat on the grounds that if anything should happen to me, you cannot face your mother. For the same reason *bhaiyya*, allow me to go with you now".

The king seemed to consider the pleading entreaty in the other's voice before replying. "It's a bad idea for both of us to expose ourselves at the same time Lakki. One never knows what Vichint is going to do and Vithalla must never be without a king. On the other hand, it will not be a bad idea to let Vichint see you. Maybe that will . . . .". The king closed his eyes now and remained lost in thought for a long minute. Finally he looked at the younger man. "Alright, Lakki. If that is what you wish. But you must go no farther than the bridge", said the king. Nor would he be persuaded, in spite of the prince's protestations, to concede anything more than that.

Within an hour, the chariot carrying them rolled out onto the bridge. Vichint had stationed himself at the other side of the bridge. He expected the expeditionary force that he had dispatched the night before to break through any moment and stood chaffing there in exasperation. There was a mild worry beginning to build up in him now at the delay. It was not a situation that was familiar to him, and his aides, gauging his mood, kept out of his way.

He scowled now as he saw the chariot. He turned to his councilor. "Who's that fool?", he asked. The old man shielded his eyes from the sun and strained to look at the figure advancing towards them. "From the description I have been given, I should think it is the king", he replied.

"In a chariot?", came the puzzled query.

Kishan Dev turned to his king with a smile. "Your majesty has not heard, perhaps, that the king of Vithalla cannot ride a horse", said the councillor.

There was an expression of incredulity stamped on the coarse features as Vichint heard the reply. "And his people send this woman to talk to me?"

A wry smile came into the old councillor's face now. "Your majesty might recall that according to the most ancient legend in this country, your heroic forbear and his four brothers were assisted in an internecine war by a low born prince of a small kingdom, whose part in that war—apart from metaphysical discourse—was confined to driving a chariot". He paused to look at the king before adding slowly, "The same legend also relates how that charioteer engineered the complete destruction—to the last man—of a mightier host than ours. In the process he outgeneraled some formidable warriors whose prowess might compare not unfavourably with even your majesty's", said Kishen Dev tactfully, as he saw a gathering frown on Vichint's face.

The king of Vithalla, meanwhile had been advancing towards them. As was his wont, he had meticulously planned and rehearsed every act of his mission—and the rehearsal had required that the prince should dismount, hand over to him a large casket which the king himself would carry, then walk towards the group gathered at the other end of the bridge. He had, with his customary thoroughness, chosen even the clothes that the prince should wear—it was a tight-fitting tunic of coarse, but light fabric, which showed the young man's formidable physique to its full advantage. Though there had been no time to explain the reason behind all this careful theatricality, it did not occur to those close to him to doubt that every gesture, every contrivance or artifice, would have a calculated purpose behind it. As king Vichint glared at the approaching figure, his lips curled in a sneer and he spat noisily.

Vithalla's king had observed the act and prepared himself for the kind of reception it portended. However, upon reaching the group of men he made a slight bow to the giant and said: "My lord, I bring with me words of peace from the people of Vithalla".

The other looked at the slight and swarthy figure standing before him with unconcealed contempt. "What are your terms for surrendering?" he asked.

Vithalla's king, disconcerted by the directness of the query, was nevertheless saved from answering this question as Kishan Dev turned tactfully to his sovereign. "Wouldn't your majesty like to go in?" They trooped into Vichint's tent slowly, with the latter himself leading the way and a number of aides bringing up the rear. As soon as they were seated, the royal visitor placed before his guest a large ornately carved wooden box that he had brought with him. "This is a gift to your royal highness from Vithalla", he said. He opened it as he was speaking, to reveal an exquisitely wrought bracelet of gold inside. He closed the box slowly and sat up and looked at the king.

"Your majesty would have heard that Vithalla's people are a peaceable folk. We have not had a war in decades in the valley itself and live in peace with each other", he began.

The lord of Bhimpur held up a huge hand as large as the head of the smaller man. "Look. If your people have the courage to come out and fight, do it now. If they don't, surrender immediately. Don't waste my time with all your noble speeches. You can reserve them for your courtiers. The valley people are a bunch of lily-livered cowards and will be slaughtered if they try to stand up to me. So tell me what terms you have brought".

The king of Vithalla's response to this was a gesture which was half way between a nod and a bow—in acknowledgement of this demand. He began talking now, slowly and clearly, never taking his eyes off his host and in a few brief words outlined the proposal which he had already placed before his council. "Your majesty will realise that we make this offer from a position of strength", he added. "Unlike the other kingdoms in the valley, ours is impregnable in its defences. There are even those in my council who feel that we have offered too much for too little. Indeed, in fact, I have a hotheaded younger brother who would fain challenge your highness to a personal combat".

"Send the young pup to me. After I carve him up, you can carry your precious prince's pieces back", said his interlocutor savagely.

"Ah yes", replied the guest. "He indeed does not know your majesty's prowess or renown. Such is the unthinking rashness of youth. But I am sure that you will realise, my lord, the variety of opinion that is ranged against me in making this offer".

Vichint massaged his massive jaw. The offer had taken him by surprise and he was not sure how he should respond.

"If it pleases your majesty, can I have a word in private?" It was Kishan Dev who spoke now. Vichint frowned at this interruption, but slowly got up and followed his councillor to an antechamber partitioned from the bigger by a thick curtain. "How is your majesty disposed towards the proposal?" he began.

Vichint snorted. "Disposed?" he echoed. "Why, I'll tie up that chamber attendant who calls himself a king, to a stake outside. I'll then torture him and then behead him in front of his people. That will teach them to lay down conditions to me".

Kishan Dev sighed. "And what does your majesty hope to achieve by the measure? If prince Lakkan Pal succeeds him for instance, do you think you will get better terms? By the way, I can confirm that story about the prince wanting to challenge you. It was common knowledge. My spies had brought me word of it".

"Do you think I'm afraid of that prince of theirs? Let him see me first *and then* we will see whether he's still prepared to challenge me".

"He *has* seen your majesty. Do you remember that young man who stood with king Ram Pal near the chariot?" The councillor gave the other a shrewdly appraising look. "Your majesty must not make the dangerous mistake of dismissing prince Lakkan Pal of Vithalla as another indolent princeling fattened upon palace pleasures". The old man was reading his sovereign's countenance like a book now. "He's a fearless young lion", he continued relentlessly. "There are stories enough about him that testify to his strength and courage. One, for instance, relates how, on one occasion, attacked by a bear when he was alone, he killed it singlehanded".

"Bring me the biggest bear you can find and I'll show you what I can do to it", came the prompt reply. The old man looked at the giant and nodded thoughtfully. "I had not quite finished", he said now. "I must tell you that the prince was not quite fourteen years old when he did it".

"You sicken me with all these stories, Kishan Dev. Half a dozen fawning courtiers can make up any number of flattering stories. I'll tell you it takes greater courage to stand up to a man than fight against a bear". For all these sneering words, the splendidly stalwart frame of the young prince rose in Vichint's mind's eye now. In a wrestling match, he knew he could prevail against anybody. But when his opponent would fight with a sword? He passed his tongue over lips that had suddenly become dry.

"Your majesty is fearless", said the old man tactfully. "I'm sure you could despatch that rash young fool. But suppose he should even scratch you, I shall be held accountable for it to the people".

"You are right", said the other thickly. "Even a superficial wound may alarm my men. It would be best to avoid any occasion for demoralising them during a campaign. If conditions had been different I would have made mincemeat of that fool", said Vichint. "Your majesty speaks wisely. But I must confess myself worried about the offer king Ram Pal has made. I fear a trap somewhere. Could the intention be to decoy us into the city and then . . ."

"And then? Are you suggesting that a bunch of fifteen hundred peasants fall on twenty five hundred of my men and slaughter them?" The king's voice held a sneering edge.

The old councilor could not help granting the truth of that appraisal and it irritated him. He looked coldly at his king. "Your majesty still does not know the fate of two thousand of our best fighting men that we sent into the kingdom yesterday", he reminded tartly. "I am worried", he continued. He nodded in the direction of the bigger room. "He knows something we don't. I don't like this", he muttered almost to himself.

"All this talking and negotiation is getting us nowhere, Kishan Dev. I say we'll wait till this evening for the men to break through. If they don't, at dawn tomorrow, we'll cross the river at the northern ford and take the city".

The councillor shook his head slowly. "It is my earnest entreaty to your majesty to do nothing in haste. King Ram Pal of Vithalla is no fool. The man is cunning as a fox and I suspect he's leading us into a trap". He paced the room for a minute before turning to his king. "If your majesty will permit me, I will go to him and ask him time till tomorrow morning to consider his offer. By then we should know what happened to the men". Vichint considered this proposal in silence for a moment before nodding reluctantly. Kishan Dev spent no further time in the king's presence. He knew he had wrested the permission to deal with the matter in his own way against the king's instincts, and saw no reason to risk its withdrawal. He had been speaking no more than the truth when he confessed himself uneasy about the disappearance of two thousand men, and had started worrying whether the intelligence he had received about the strength of Vithalla's army could have been wrong.

Accordingly, he returned to the room where the parleys had been conducted and in as few words as possible intimated to his guest that a decision would be communicated on the morrow. Upon this the latter immediately withdrew.

CHAPTER 26

A KING AND HIS COUNCIL

On reaching the palace king Ram Pal found his own council in session and waiting anxiously for him. There had been an air of jubilation in the court and among the people when the fate of Vichint's advance guard had been made known. In less than an hour of engagement, Vichint had lost two thousand men, without a single casualty on the defenders' side. "The fact there has been no report of the missing men, I feel, is causing considerable unease there", the king revealed. "I think that was one reason why they have asked for time. Before they decide what to do with my offer, they must know the fate of their campaign. Its outcome is certainly going to affect that decision materially".

"Does your majesty intend the news of their being taken prisoner to be released yet?" asked Verma anxiously. He had been advocating that the invading army be kept in the dark about the capture as long as it was possible. And when he heard his king affirm the demoralising effect it was having on the enemy, he felt his strategy amply vindicated. It was with astonishment, therefore, that he received his king's reply. "I am hoping I can persuade you not only to release the news, but the prisoners, too", the king declared.

If it was anxiety that Verma had felt, it was plain dismay now. "But . . . Surely your majesty can see that nothing prevents the enemy from throwing them into battle against us once more?" The king could see that the argument had the assembly impressed.

"I'll give you two reasons for my move", he said. "The first is, that it is my hope that everything we do now should be towards discouraging the enemy from continuing this war".

"And by releasing the prisoners they will stop the war?" It was the prince now who asked the question, with incredulity in his voice.

"That brings me to my second reason, Lakki. I want you to imagine the impact these released prisoners are going to have on the rest. I don't mean merely the fact of their disastrous campaign coming to light. But I would like to remind you of a few facts. Vichint had thrown two thousand of presumably their best warriors at us last night. They have been ambushed and virtually destroyed by *four hundred and fifty archers.* Remember that's all the number we could spare, since I had to dispatch about the same number to the southern ford, in case Vichint had planned on a pincer movement. It's fortunate for us, of course, that in my lord Vichint, we have a man who does not plan anything. But I'll come back again to the soldiers that we are going to send back. Imagine the story they are going to take back. They are *not* going to tell a man like their king that they were massacred by a handful of archers. The version they will give is that they were outnumbered ten to one and had no chance.

At the least, Vichint will be told that there were not less than ten thousand men guarding the breach on that side. It would then stand to reason that we would have that many men at least at a number of other places along the wall. And the trenches that we have dug would be made out to be huge moats, wide and long. The ramparts would become steep and unscaleable walls. The breaches in the walls we were so worried about would be represented as fiendish traps from where lethal ambushes would be sprung. Half of these would be imagined and the rest made up. But in the face of such daunting accounts, we will have to see how many of Vichint's army, many of whom are mercenaries whose primary object is the prospect of some easy plunder, would be enthusiastic about participating in an attack against the city".

An hour later, an eerie silence descended on the eastern bank of the Vajravallabha as the remnant of Vichint's expeditionary force slowly made its way across the bridge. Less than half the men who had set out had returned. Of these, hundreds were dying or seriously wounded and permanently disabled. They were being helped along by their comrades, some of them being carried on shoulders.

CHAPTER 27

PEACE RETURNS

As the sun sank on that day, the king and his younger brother personally supervised the deployment of the defending forces near the southern and northern points in the wall at which they expected a nocturnal attack. It was an anxious and unblinking vigil they kept that night. But the morning broke with serenity and birdsong. Relieved, the brothers returned to the palace from opposite directions. And found the palace and its surroundings agog. Scouts had reported that Vichint's mighty host was nowhere in sight. The king, with his brother, hurried immediately to the bridge to find that the invaders had indeed vanished in the night. Could it be a ploy to lull the defenders into security before striking at them? Scouts were again dispatched. There could be no doubt this time. The dust from the retreating army could be seen far to the east. Finally, the reason that put that formidable army to precipitate flight was pieced together from those who had been too badly wounded to move with their more fortunate brethren. The previous evening the news of the meeting between the two kings and the strange offer made by Vithalla's king had leaked out. Shortly after that the rumour had spread like wildfire through the camp: the kingdom of Vithalla was in the grip of a deadly epidemic of plague for which there was no known cure. Two of the men who had returned from that disastrous expedition had died and their bodies had turned black, it went. And Vithalla's offer was a stratagem to decoy the king and his men inside the city walls. None who entered would come out of that city of the dead.

The rumour was apparently all that the army, demoralised by the carnage of their advance guard and dispirited by the prospect of a long siege needed to break them. The mercenaries were the first to melt away quietly. It did not take long for the reminder of Vichint's men, always lacking in discipline, to join them and turn that initial flight of a few into an ignominious rout. In an unbelievable twinkling of an eye, the wind of a rumour had blown away the scourge from the north.

The brothers had crossed the bridge and gone out to inspect for themselves the site where the formidable host had been camped scarce a day before. As they were returning, the prince who had been silent the while, now turned to his brother, a bewildered expression on his face. "I don't believe all this is happening", he said.

The king nodded in assent. "This country has suffered grievously in the past through untold calamities. Maybe the Guardian Spirits of Vithalla, whoever they are, had decided finally that some compensation was in order".

"It must be so, *bhaiyya*, if they can make an army the size of Vichint's, imagine disease and blackened bodies and make them flee". The king was silent for a while, then gave his brother a long look. "I did not say anything about anybody imagining something like that, Lakki", he said slowly.

The younger man looked at the king with a frown. "But didn't you hear what the men just told you? They did say clearly that they saw the blackened bodies, didn't they?"

"I heard it, Lakki. I'm not saying they imagined the *bodies*. Those were real enough. The imagination came in when they believed that their comrades died of some mysterious disease".

The prince looked at his brother again. "I don't believe I understand you, when you start talking like that", he said.

"I'll tell you what I mean, Lakki. But keep what I'm going to say now to yourself. Take me on trust when I say that there are compelling reasons why it shouldn't go any farther". The king looked at his younger brother, who nodded uncertainly. "First, I got four or five versions of what happened, and there were significant discrepancies between them. In one, for instance, the two dead men came into Vithalla with the expedition that forded the river and sneaked in. In another, the bodies of the men *were discovered by their comrades and carried back to camp*. Discovered where? Here again, there were further discrepancies. According to what I believe to be the most reliable version, a group of half a dozen of Vichint's men had crossed the Vajravallabha at some point downriver.

They must have used a narrow rope bridge whose existence I had quite forgotten about. The purpose, however, is not clear. They might have been sent on a spying mission by that wily old councilor of Vichint's—Kishan Dev. Or, it might have been merely a private hunting expedition. I have some reason to suspect it was the latter. Anyway, if they had crossed by the rope bridge, they would have found themselves at the foot of the hills".

The king paused. "After that, it becomes a matter of conjecture. Let us say they got into the mountains to hunt and then got separated. Or possibly they split into two groups and agreed to meet again at the bridge at the appointed time. And when that time comes and two of them do not turn up, their comrades go in search of them and find their blackened bodies, which they carry back to camp".

The narration stopped now as the king seemed to be occupied with his thoughts. The prince, after waiting expectantly for the account to continue and finding him silent, asked: "If they did not die of disease, how did the bodies turn black?"

"Can you think of any other reason besides disease, that turns bodies black, Lakki? And remember that there is no known disease which kills in a few hours".

The prince looked with puzzlement at his brother. "They did not die of disease, Lakki. Can you imagine their comrades carrying to the camp the bodies of two men whom they thought to have died of a mysterious disease which could kill in a matter of hours". The king shook his head. "They were charred by *fire*, Lakki".

As the prince turned uncomprehending eyes towards his brother, the meaning of what the latter was saying suddenly dawned on him. He gaped at the king with astonishment. "You mean . . .", he stopped, an unbelieving expression on his face.

The latter nodded. "They must have gone into the mountains to hunt and must have made the fatal error of stalking something which killed much more surely and swiftly than a wolf or a bear, or indeed anything in their experience", said the king thoughtfully.

An year later, spring had come again with its customary loveliness to the land. It had also been an year of relative peace and quiet consolidation that the king could look back on with some satisfaction. The vision he had had for his country was gradually taking shape and the social institutions necessary for bringing it about had already been initiated. A tax system that was rational and more humane had been drawn up and schools that would serve as the nursery of a corps of civil servants had been established. It would have taken a generation, of course, for the social benefits of enlightenment to start making itself manifest; but the king believed that the movement towards reform had built up an irresistible momentum that would carry it forward. And with that realisation, his mind began to turn back to the thoughts of Nalanda and the ultimate relinquishment of power to his younger brother.

In fact, as soon as the threat of the army at the gates of Vithalla had been fortuitously withdrawn, he had decided the time had come to sound out the prince's views on the matter. Accordingly, as the first step towards its accomplishment, the series of royal edicts that had been promulgated bringing in sweeping changes of policy, had all been issued in the prince's name. When the latter had enquired about the necessity for this unusual procedure, the king had told him that the time had come for the prince to accept a larger role in first shaping and then guiding the destiny of his country. The explanation was deliberately vague. The king had hoped that by a series of such subtle signals, the prince would be prepared to accept the plans that had been made for him, when the time came for the disclosure of it to be made. The deeper purpose behind the king's decision in having the prince announce the reformative measures, indeed, was to secure for him the gratitude and goodwill that the knowledge generated among the populace.

All this, though, had not been achieved without resistance from entrenched enclaves of hereditary privilege, of course. Some of the nobles and their families had realised by this time the direction the reforms were taking and the personal implications of the overhaul of the power structure and how their own standing in it would be marginalised.

It was here that Vichint's attempted invasion began to have an effect that was as decisive as it was unexpected. For, the way the king had marshalled the slender defence resources of his country against a foe that had brutally outnumbered it, had enhanced his stature in the eyes of his people. There was a spirit abroad now among them which, if it could not be called assertiveness yet, was certainly a state of awakening that promised to lead to that state. And those who stood against the reforms the king had initiated, suddenly found themselves obliged to reckon with a force which had hitherto remained of negligible significance in any attempt aimed at altering the power hierarchy—namely, the stature of the individual initiating it and his standing with the subjects who were its beneficiaries.

On the other hand, there was also a reason why an armed insurrection was not a valid option. Sanathan's shrewd observation that the morale of the army was good, though made in the context of its ability to withhold a limited external aggression, was certainly a correct assessment as regards its capacity to deal effectively with civil unrest. This perception was furthered by the well-known personal loyalty of the General to his sovereign. Thus it came about that while the king's attempts to redress the abuse of traditional privilege, while far from being universally accepted, did not meet with the kind of resolute and concerted armed resistance, or even the threat of it, that might have obliged him to withdraw them, or even reconsider his policy.

CHAPTER 28

"WOULD YOU LIKE TO BE
THE KING?"

It was a bright, moonlit night and the king had brought his brother to walk along the familiar route that led to the clearing on the hilltop. It had become something of a custom with the king to seek the peace and solitude of the little glade whenever he had anything important to say to the prince.

He had begun by talking about the changes that had been brought about in the year that had gone and what remained to be done. "After the experience we have had with Vichint's army last year, I think the kingdoms in the region will be receptive to the idea of a confederacy—a loose association under which they will agree to meet any threat from an aggressor collectively. It is my desire to send you to discuss this matter with the the kingdoms in this region".

"The idea being yours, I thought you would be better suited to the task", said the prince. The king seemed to be considering this before replying.

"I think the rulers of the kingdoms in the valley will have to come to know you. Also, Tham will go with you. You will find him an extremely sharp person who will be able to advise you soundly on matters of statecraft". He paused. "Do you know he has decided to settle in Vithalla?", he asked.

The other nodded. "I guessed as much when he did not leave with some of the others who had come with him, though I must consider myself surprised by his decision". The king shook his head. "You should not be, Lakki. Every man has a proper sphere. Maybe you do not know he is going to marry Verma's daughter?" The king could see clearly that the news had again caught the other by surprise. The prince smiled now. "I think there are a lot of things I need to learn about people", he said.

"It's what I was saying about one's proper sphere of life, Lakki. He has recognized his, that's all". After a short pause he added: "And I know mine".

The prince looked at him quickly. "Well, then. I think I don't know *you* well enough either", he said. "I thought you were one of those people who would think kingship a tiresome obligation".

If the king noticed the prince's misinterpretation of his words, he however gave no sign of it. "What about you Lakki? Would you like being king?" he asked now.

The other did not answer immediately. They had reached the clearing by this time and sat down in the grass.

The moon shone through the trees. In another two days it would be full, thought the king. "I've thought over that question, *bhaiyya*. There were times when I thought you were about to ask me that question".

"You are very perceptive, Lakki. Answer my question now". There was again a pause. The moon shone full on the young man's face and the king could see he looked disturbed. The latter turned now to face the older man squarely, as if he had reached a decision. "I think I would welcome the prospect. That is, of course, if you wanted me to be the king. But I still cannot help feeling ashamed about it".

"I never expected you to be less than honest, Lakki. I'm grateful to you for that. And there's nothing to be ashamed about it. I had an old teacher once who used to tell me that nothing qualified a person for kingship as his distaste for it. I think I imbibed a lot of my attitudes from him. But I do not entirely agree with him on that observation". He was silent now. "I think you know why I brought you here, Lakki". The other nodded slowly.

"It is my wish that you should become the ruler of Vithalla. Soon, after consulting our mother, I intend making an announcement to that effect. Your people will be fortunate to have you as king. And I know you well enough to know that you will use your power with wisdom".

"With you to guide me that will not be difficult, *bhaiyya*". The king seemed to be thinking this over.

"My presence will not be necessary, Lakki. You will have to learn to be your own man". "What do you mean by that?" exclaimed the young man. The king could detect alarm in his voice.

"I'll tell you about the plans I have made for myself, later. What I'm going to do will be the best for both of us".

CHAPTER 29

AN INVITATION

There was silence between them now as each of them became absorbed in his own thoughts. It must have lasted for sometime when the king finally decided that they had stayed long enough. He was about to get up when he noticed that the prince was staring at something behind him. The prince's hand reached out to touch him softly on the forearm. "Behind you, *bhaiyya*. Slowly".

There was an edge in the young man's voice. As the king turned around slowly to look behind him, he knew what he would find. Three of the creatures were standing there. Two of them were in the edge of the clearing. In their hands they carried the tube that the king had seen earlier and he guessed that it was some kind of weapon. It was, however, on the third figure that his eyes fastened on now. The creature had advanced a few feet in front of the other two and the king could see that it was unarmed. It was gazing into his eyes now and the king could feel a tingling in his mind, as if it was being stroked lightly by some process he was at a loss to understand.

Suddenly words and pictures began to take shape and swim in his mind, unlike anything he had ever experienced. He realized that the creature was communicating with him. Slowly, haltingly, the words began to form. After the first few confused thoughts, the jumble began to come into focus. "Both of you . . . Both of you . . . in two days . . . must come . . . must come . . . here . . . vitally important . . . come . . . here . . . two days . . . vitally . . . important . . . If you fail . . . . forfeit . . . . everything . . . ." The words were coming in bursts now. The king realized that the creature was waiting for him to respond—some sign from him in order to know it was reaching him. "Two of you . . . Come alone . . . . Vitally important . . . . vitally important . . . ." The bursts went now.

He made a supreme effort to think—to convey his thoughts somehow to the creature who stood before him. "We will come", he said and found to his surprise that he was speaking aloud. "Surely". He had no way of knowing whether he was reaching the creature or not. For a moment there were no movement from anybody. Then the creature turned back and slowly returned to where its companions were standing. In an instant they had disappeared into the darkness of the trees.

The two men stood there for some time, uncertain about what they should do. Then the king turned to the younger man. "Come, Lakki", he said. "I don't think any purpose is to be served by standing here any longer".

They turned slowly and went back the way they had come. The prince was the first to speak. "What is it *Bhaiyya*? What happened? You seemed to be saying something to it". "Tell me something, Lakki. Did you hear anything? I mean, did you feel somebody was trying to talk to you?"

The prince looked at him in astonishment. "Is that what was happening? Were you conversing with each other then?"

"I don't know", replied the king in bewilderment. "Something was certainly happening in my mind". He told him then about the words that had come into his mind. "It is possible that it was saying something to me in this fashion. It seemed to be a repeated message of some sort that we must come here again in two days. If we don't. Well, there seemed to be a warning that we lose something valuable. I think it used the word 'forfeit'. It was trying to tell us that something very important to us was going to happen here in two days and that if we are not here then, we would pay a heavy price for it". They walked along in silence for some time.

"What shall we do, *Bhaiyya*?"

"Why, I think we will come here on the appointed day. Somehow, I am inclined to believe the creature", said the king.

"But what if it's a trap?" asked the other.

The king seemed to think it over. "They could have done what they wanted with us even now, Lakki. They don't have to wait for another two days and trap us if what they wanted was to do away with us. No, no, Lakki. It's something else that we can have no idea about". He looked at his younger brother. "Like to find out, Lakki?"

And so on a full moon day, when an argent flood was loosed over the valley, the king and his brother stood waiting in the clearing. They had come alone, as they had been instructed. To their mother they had told as much as was strictly necessary and to the court and its officials, they let it be known that they may be gone for a day or more. It was strange waiting there, not knowing what was going to happen, thought the king. That the situation carried a certain risk, he could not deny, in spite of what he had told the prince. The bright disc was climbing into the sky. It was near its zenith before their vigil was rewarded.

There was a movement towards the far end and one of the creatures came out slowly. It was looking unblinkingly at them as it lurched towards them with slow, short and ungainly steps. The king could see that it was attended by half a dozen of the others who stood behind it without moving, near the farther edge of the clearing. When the creature was about ten paces away from them, it stopped. It looked more than ever like a four foot high bat, thought the king. The creature raised the arm like appendages it had at its sides, carefully folded them and put them over its chest, looking at him the while. Sound suddenly issued from its mouth. "Challoni", it said. The sound came slurred with a sibilant shrillness. The king guessed that it was telling him what it was called. He now imitated the creature's action and, placing his hands on his chest intoned his own name as clearly as he could. It stood unmoving, looking at him with its fixed and oddly disconcerting gaze. It then turned its back to the men, extended its arms towards its companions and repeated slowly: "Challoni". The king realized now that it was telling him that the creature was referring to its own species in this fashion.

It then turned back towards them with laborious effort, careful not to unbalance and then brought its hands together as it had done earlier, but now held them at a distance of half a foot in front of it, in a gesture oddly reminiscent of indicating. "Selzi", it said. The king now understood that it was introducing itself, and nodded. It occurred to him that his own gesture might not mean anything to the other. It began talking again, slowly, in what the king recognized to be the language of the shepherds of the region. "You . . . will . . . go . . . with . . . us . . . You . . . saved . . . my . . . life . . . and . . . we . . . wish . . . to . . . do . . . something . . . for . . . you . . . in . . . return". There was a pause. "We . . . hope . . . you . . . will . . . be . . . able . . . to . . . use . . . what . . . we . . . are . . . going . . . to . . . give . . . you . . . to . . . save . . . your . . . species".

CHAPTER 30

THE JOURNEY

As the words ceased, the two men looked at the creature in blank astonishment. However, before they could ask what it meant, it had raised its arms and gestured that they should follow it. They left the glade now with the two men walking a few paces behind. They made slow progress. The king was not sure about the direction they were going in, but they could see that they were descending. From the position of the moon, the two men calculated that they had been proceeding for about two hours in this fashion, when the group ahead of them finally halted. When the men had caught up with them, one of the goblins walked up to a big rock. It stood there for a minute and stooped over a point on the rock about two feet from the ground and seemed to be doing something to its surface. Presently, a section of the rock face seemed to swing inward to reveal an opening about five feet high. The rock must have been hollowed inside, decided the king, as a flood of illumination poured out from inside it. The creature which had introduced itself as Selzi now entered through the aperture that had been opened, where it was joined by two of its companions. Selzi now turned to the two men and uttered the single word: "Come".

When the men entered the interior, they found it to be large enough to hold five men. The inner walls appeared to be made of a smooth, hard, white shell. The creatures conversed in low tones now, while the men were taking stock of the chamber in which they found themselves. On the opposite side to where the men stood was a table and on it a screen. The screen came alive now with a sequence of flashing lights. Selzi came to them now ; "Please . . . stand . . . against . . . the . . . wall . . . do . . . not . . . worry . . . about . . . these . . . formalities . . . it . . . is . . . for . . . your . . . own . . . good".

As the men did as they were asked, Selzi pulled out two metallic strips from a slit in the wall, on either side of the men and fastened the ends together. They found that they were now strapped to the wall by a band between their knee and ankle. This procedure was now repeated with two other strips, one around their middle and another at the level of their chest. Selzi had to mount a small step-ladder to fasten the last two belts. With the three straps in place, they found they had completely lost their mobility. The king turned to smile reassuringly at his younger brother. "I don't think there's any need to worry, Lakki", he said. The young man smiled back a little uncertainly. One of the creatures who had been watching the display of lights at the screen, now turned to Selzi and said something. There was an exchange of words between them, upon which the former began to ascend by what appeared to be a small stair that spiralled up the side of the wall. Presently he disappeared through a trapdoor in the ceiling into what must have been a smaller chamber above.

Selzi now returned to the two men. "We will now be leaving on a long journey. During the entire duration of it, it will be necessary to suspend your awareness to your surroundings. As far as you are concerned, it will be sinking into sleep. You will wake up again in surroundings which will be entirely unfamiliar to you. You should not allow any of these things to bother you; in particular, remember that your capacity for judgement should not be impaired. Once we reach the place which is our destination, the entire purpose of the journey will be revealed to you. Till then you will have to be patient. In fact, any further information that we can give you will be useless to you, since you will not be able to understand it. Do you wish to know anything else regarding your journey?"

"No", said the king.

"Then just relax now. You will enter a pleasant sleep like state", said Selzi. It mounted the step ladder again and brought what seemed like a large, round vessel near their faces. The men felt a vapour escaping from it. It seemed to swirl around them as a pleasant and fragrant mist. That was the last sensation they had before their consciousness left them.

When their senses returned, they found that they were loosely supported by their straps. Selzi was standing before them and watching them. At a gesture from it, two of its companions came forward and removed the straps. It seemed to the king that they had lost a large part of their weight and become much lighter. Selzi confirmed this fact. "But you will soon adjust yourself to this altered condition", they were told. "Come with me now", the goblin intoned and led the way out of the shell through the door. When they stepped out, Selzi stopped to let them look around them at their new surroundings. Fully prepared as they were to find themselves in a place which would be strange and unfamiliar—which would bear no recognisable feature related to their own experience—they were nevertheless stunned at the spectacle that greeted them on emerging.

For, it was not the rock that they stepped out of. They found themselves standing on a platform attached to the hard white shell, which itself was standing on three supporting metal fins. Gone was the forest, the trees and the moonlight. Light there was—it was a diffused pearly glow coming from lamps which seemed to be hanging from the sky. On closer inspection the king decided that they were standing under a vast transparent dome of some unknown material and the lamps were attached to it. By shielding his eyes against the lights and straining them, he could see, above the dome, a night sky pricked with the diamond lights of stars. His heart began to beat faster at the sight. He stood there now, rapt in that vision and searching for the familiar constellations. He could see the constellation of the seven sages as were some other constellations that he could recognise; but the pole star was gone, while a number of unfamiliar lights crowded on to that celestial screen.

Selzi had been waiting patiently while the king was conducting his survey of the spangled vastness above. When the king turned his attention back to his companions, Selzi now went to the edge of the platform and jumped off and looked expectantly at the two men. The platform was at a height of four feet from the ground. The prince now stepped to the edge of the platform and jumped a trifle apprehensively. To his surprise, he landed with a soft thud. The ground seemed to be made of rocks and dust. The king now followed suit. With Selzi leading the way, they walked towards a group of structures a little distance away. Indeed, the area under the dome contained several buildings, big and small. They now arrived at the door of what appeared to be a small room. Their host opened the door for them and entered behind them. The men found themselves in a chamber which had obviously been prepared for their residence. Selzi pointed to a small button like protuberance on the wall. "If you need anything you can press that", he said. "One of us will come to you who will be able to communicate with you. You are free to go wherever you like and learn whatever you want to know about this place. But there are just three of us here who can communicate with you in your language. I will arrange food to be sent to you. In a few hours time, I will call on you to explain the purpose of this visit to you. Till then I suggest you take some rest. If you need anything, you can let us know immediately". Selzi now closed the door softly and left.

CHAPTER 31

A STRANGE PLACE

The prince looked at his brother. "Is all this really happening, or am I dreaming, *Bhaiyya?*"

The king smiled. "I know exactly what you mean, Lakki. I find it difficult to shake off a feeling of unreality, myself". He wandered around the room, examining everything. "I would like to take Selzi's invitation to look around for what it's worth, Lakki. Maybe we can learn something about this strange place".

They went out now and started wandering around aimlessly, going where their fancy took them. Everywhere, their presence attracted curious stares from the creatures. The king started speaking. "Let me summarise whatever I have understood about this situation, Lakki, if only to clarify it in my mind. *First, Selzi is no creature of the Earth.* They are a species who call themselves the Challoni. I don't think they are going to let us know anything more about themselves. They have been on Earth for at least fifty years now and I have a feeling that they have been here for considerably longer than that. But we know nothing about their purpose. They are obviously at a much more advanced stage of knowledge and technology than ourselves". The king stopped now and seemed to be marshalling his thoughts.

"The rock that we got into was no rock They have cunningly disguised that egg shaped object that we rescued them from. That was why we were not able to find any trace of it after that incident. And it is in that machine that we have travelled here".

The prince looked at him. "That means that . . . ." The young man left the sentence unfinished and looked at the king, an expression of alarm spreading over his countenance.

"That we are no longer on Earth? Almost certainly, no. I realized that as soon as I saw the position of the stars in the sky overhead. In fact we must be very far from our planet, Lakki. How far, I have no means of knowing. If I had to venture an opinion, I would say we are adrift in a sea of space on one of thousands upon thousands of points of light that we see every day in the night sky. Or it may even be a comet or a planet of whose existence we are ignorant of till now". The king stopped and glanced frowningly up at the sky. "That brings us to two unanswered questions. The first is, why have we been brought here? Whatever the reason is, I am sure they mean us no harm. With the powers that they can command, it is absurd to think that they should bring us all the way here merely to despatch us". The king shook his head in frustration. "Nothing seems to make sense", he said finally.

"What is the second question?" asked the prince. "The second is no less puzzling. If the first is about the place we are in, the second is the time. Is there any significance in bringing us here *at this time?* After all, they could have brought us here earlier or later—or, for that matter, any time they wanted. Remember that we come to the glade almost every week. I can't help thinking that the Challoni have arranged the timing of this expedition with care".

By now their wandering had brought them to a large hall one side of which was closed off with a transparent partition. They could look through it into the lit interior, where bank upon bank of fantastically wrought instruments stood. On an impulse, the king pushed the door open and entered. There was nobody inside. He walked around, looking at the instruments carefully. What captured the king's attention more than anything else was a system of long gleaming tubes, one fitting within the other, with the slenderest in the lowest position, a few feet from the floor. The tubes were joined together in segments, with the largest going up through an opening in the ceiling. The king was inspecting the apparatus with an absorbed fascination which the prince was loth to break into. He stood to one side now and waited patiently for the other to finish his examination.

"What was it, *Bhaiyya?*", he asked curiously when the king joined him. "I am not quite sure", said the king with a smile. "But they reminded me of something I heard about at Nalanda".

"Oh", said the prince, "you must have used them when you are at Nalanda".

The king's smile grew broader now. "I don't think human beings are going to set eyes on instruments like these for a very, very long time, Lakki. Maybe not for hundreds of years".

They reached their quarters now. They were exhausted and the physical necessity for sleep could be no longer denied. They lay on the floor which seemed to be some sort of spongy carpet and were soon sound asleep. When the king woke, he found the younger man sitting up. "While you were sleeping, somebody brought this", he said, indicating a container. The king found it contained a pink coloured fluid. He discovered it was sweet, with a tingling taste to it. On a plate there were some fruits and a kind of unleavened bread eaten by shepherds. The king drew the prince's attention to this last item. "Do you see what I meant, Lakki? The Challoni must have taken pains to study the ways and customs of the people around them—in this case, the shepherds. They must have acquired an extensive lore about them, in fact, if they can even speak their language".

CHAPTER 32

THE BOON

Shortly after they had finished eating, Selzi appeared. "Do you require anything else?" it asked. When the king replied in the negative, it addressed him again. "Come with me then. There are things which we would like to tell you". The goblin led the way to where a large carpet had been spread on the ground. Around it were sitting half a dozen of the creatures. Selzi joined the group and motioned the men to be seated likewise.

When they had settled themselves, Selzi began to speak. "We must offer you an apology for bringing you here without explaining our purpose in doing so. It was necessary to bring you here without further loss of time and any further explanations would have delayed us. First, all of us . . . we . . . would like to express our gratitude to you for saving our life. It is our intention to give you something of great value, in return for what you have done for us. Accordingly, it is our . . . my . . . intention to keep you here for another day. During that time you will be our honoured guests. At the end of that time . . . ." Selzi's narration trailed off into silence. A wordless look passed between it and one of the creatures. There was a silence that lasted a few minutes, before Selzi continued. "At the end of that time, you will decide what you want".

There was another silence now. As the prince began to speak, Selzi held up a hand for silence. This time the silence was longer. It was a weird ceremony, the king thought, the way the creatures just stopped abruptly while speaking.

As abruptly as it had stopped, Selzi began speaking again. "We would like you to understand clearly the terms of the offer that is being made to you, so that you may use it to your maximum benefit. I will, therefore, repeat it at length in detail. You are free to move around this place and look at everything. Nothing that you want to see will be denied access to you. Anything that you can set your eyes on and which you would like to have will be yours, provided it is within . . . my . . . our power to give it to you, of course. You have, therefore, a whole day to make up your mind and tell us what you want. At the end of it you will be taken back to Earth. To facilitate this process, we would like you to move around my township and see everything. We hope you will make a wise choice. But whatever your choice, the responsibility will be entirely yours". The flow of the words ceased as Selzi sank into one of its by now customary silences. When it started speaking again, it was to say: "For certain reasons which we cannot explain, I . . . we . . . Selzi stopped in seeming confusion. "We . . . that is, I", it continued, "cannot answer any questions which are not directly concerned with the offer and its terms I am making". Another silence fell again.

CHAPTER 33

A Tour

This time, after a few minutes, the Challoni rose together like one entity, bowed towards their guests and then started walking away. After a slight hesitation, the men, realising that the Challoni had communicated whatever they had wanted to say, likewise started to walk back to their quarters. Neither of them spoke till they had reached it. The prince turned towards his brother then. "What are you thinking of, *Bhaiyya?*" he asked. The king did not reply. When the younger man repeated the question, however, he seemed to shake himself out of a trance. "There are certain things about the Challoni that I have begun to notice. In fact, I should have seen this earlier". He sighed now. "But I'm no closer to answering my two questions".

"What is it you have observed about the Challoni, *Bhaiyya?*" asked the prince.

"Did you observe how Selzi seemed to sink into silences every few minutes?" The prince nodded. "That suggested something to me", said the king. "I wonder whether you observed another interesting thing about Selzi. It seemed to be confused when it had to use the word 'I' or 'We'. It kept interchanging them, unnecessarily it seemed to me, and sometimes stumbled over the words. Also, remember that Selzi does not appear to be the chief or leader or even a prominent member of the group. So that we are apparently being rewarded for saving a perfectly ordinary member. All this made me suspect something about the Challoni. But I won't talk any more about it now. I need some more time".

"In that case, why not accept Selzi's invitation and take another sightseeing trip around this place?" asked the prince.

"Certainly", replied the king. "I was about to suggest that myself".

As they were going out, they were intercepted by Selzi. "I thought I would show you something of the things we do here. Can you come with me?"

They followed the waddling little figure ahead of them. It led them straight to a huge hall much larger than the one in which they had seen the instruments. There was a large table in the middle of it. The king now saw several tubes there like the ones he had seen the creatures carrying earlier. By the side of the table, near the wall was a much larger one fashioned from a strange metal the king had not seen before. It was resting on a small platform. As they approached it some of the Challoni who had been standing near it now wheeled it into position. As the men watched, the huge metal cylinder was slowly moved, apparently by a machinery they could not understand. Selzi now bade them come with him. They were taken to the far end of the hall which must have been about a hundred yards away from the cylinder. Selzi now handed over to the prince a large rock about the size of a man's head. It would have normally cost even the prince some effort, thought the king, to hold that rock, powerful as he was. But in the conditions of weightlessness in which they found themselves, he held it apparently effortlessly in one hand. Selzi now asked him to place the rock on a small tray which was supported by a metal column. It now motioned the men to stand back. "Look at the rock now", it told the brothers. Then it turned to one of the creatures which had standing expectantly near the metal cannon. There was now a sound like the crack of a whip, or a snapping twig and the rock disappeared. The men noted there was a small heap of blackened powder on the tray and a faint smell as of something being burnt.

"The rock has been vapourised by intense heat", Selzi matter-of-factly informed his dumbstruck audience. "We could destroy anything we wished to, even if it were a few miles away. The tubes you have seen us carry, in fact, have the same kind of power; but they are not quite as powerful, nor is their range as much as that of the cannon's you have seen. But come with me. There are other things you should see". The goblin led the way to another section of the great chamber. They came to a place where there was a large screen. In front of it, on a low table two feet from the ground, was a board with an array of buttons on it. At a touch, the screen came alive with figures and pictures which were incomprehensible to the men. Selzi now turned to them. "Life in this small city is regulated by machines which are controlled by the buttons you see on this panels", it said.

CHAPTER 34

"There Is Danger, Lakki"

And so it went on. To the bemused men it seemed to be a tour of miracle and magic. Its effect was to strike speech from them, so that it was only sometime after they had returned to their living quarters that they could talk about what they had seen. "I don't know about you, *Bhaiyya*. But as for myself, I know what I want from this place", said the prince.

"The killing tubes?" enquired the older man.

The prince nodded. "Just imagine what we could have done with them when Vichint came calling to our gate, *Bhaiyya*".

"I know what you mean, Lakki. The idea occurred to me too". He fell silent now. "Do you know what I think, Lakki?" He looked at his brother. "I think the whole object of today's excursion was to impress us with the power of their armaments. In other words, I think that after seeing the demonstration today, it is their armaments we were expected to ask for". He was speaking slowly now, gathering together ideas in his mind. "*There is something else much more valuable here, Lakki, that they do not want us to see*".

"But I don't understand you, *Bhaiyya*. If they don't want us to see it . . . ."

"Why show it at all?" interrupted the king. "The only answer to that question that I can think of that makes sense to me is that their sense of fairness and justice would oblige them to keep it in plain sight"

The prince looked at him quickly as his brother stopped suddenly in the middle a sentence. The latter was staring absently at some faraway thing, totally absorbed in the rapt contemplation of some idea that must have suddenly struck him, the prince decided. He shook his head then, as if to rid himself of some worrisome obsession and started speaking. "I've seen conjurors performing tricks, Lakki. Usually they work by diverting our attention away from some crucial action they are unobtrusively performing. What is going on here is a conjuring trick. We are being shown wonderful and marvellous things, while something of vital importance is being ignored by us. That tour that we were taken on is the performance of a master illusionist". He stopped and closed his eyes.

"There is danger, Lakki. Something is happening which I cannot understand".

The prince seemed to consider this for a moment. "I must confess I find it difficult to understand you, *Bhaiyya*. It was you who pointed out to me that if the Challoni intended any harm to us, they could have done it without bringing us all the way here".

The king looked at him thoughtfully. "I don't mean any physical danger to you and me merely, Lakki. It's something much bigger than that. I cannot believe for a moment that the Challoni have anything to gain by killing or harming us. It's a larger end they have in view, and I believe that we are somehow in the way of their attaining it".

"You may be right, *Bhaiyya*. On the other hand they may have nothing more in mind than rewarding us for saving one of them". There was, in the prince's tone, a hint of an impatience that the king had never heard before. Whatever reply he had fashioned in mind, he therefore thought better of expressing it and chose to remain quiet. "For myself", continued the young man, "under the circumstances, I don't think we can do any better than to examine how best to profit from the offer that has been made to us by the Challoni. I believe it is a generous offer, *Bhaiyya*". He stopped then added: "I'll be honest, *Bhaiyya*. I've set my heart on those spitfire tubes. I cannot get them out of my mind since the moment I saw them. If you and I can each carry away even an armful of those tubes from here, we would not have to fear any foe on Earth".

The king nodded absently. "Any foe on Earth . . .", he echoed softly.

"What did you say?" asked the prince.

The older man sighed. "Nothing, Lakki. Something occurred to me, when you said that, that's all". But whatever it was that was bothering the king, this clear delineation of his own position seemed to have set the young man's mind at rest, for he lay down and was soon fast asleep. The king looked long and thoughtfully at the sleeping figure. "Any foe on Earth . . .", he repeated to himself again, slowly.

He remained lost in thought for a long time. Then, apparently coming to a decision, he noiselessly went out of the room. He waited for a few minutes for his eyes to get used to the dim light outside. Most of the lights had been switched off and there was nobody in sight. The Challoni seemed to be observing Earth timings and must be in bed, decided the king. He walked slowly now, passing as much as it was possible in the shadow of the buildings. Proceeding in this fashion he finally reached the place where he had inspected the instruments in the hall. After looking around him, he softly entered the chamber and inspected its interior. There was nobody there. He stood in the darkness of the chamber and looked outside. Nothing seemed to be moving. He cautiously started pressing one after another a number of buttons on a panel, till at a touch, a light came on, and he waited for another few minutes. He seemed to have attracted no attention. He now started examining the instruments carefully, one after another. Some of those he arranged together and surveyed what he had constructed. He moved around now, absorbed in his work, and after a time, became oblivious to his surroundings. After an hour, he finally straightened up frowningly from his labours and remained wrapped in thought. He turned around to go then and was about to switch off the light when he froze with astonishment. Selzi was standing just outside the chamber, in the shadow of the doorway, to one side, looking at him with its disconcertingly unblinking gaze.

The next morning, the prince woke to find his elder brother sitting up. "Didn't you get any sleep, *Bhaiyya?*" he asked with concern.

The king shook his head. "I can sleep later, Lakki", he replied. "For now, I am too disturbed to sleep".

"I suppose that means that you have not been able to answer the questions that have been tormenting you".

"No Lakki, I have not. If anything, they are more clamorous now, as the time nears for us to make our choice".

"Have you learned anything new about the matter then, that disturbs you?" asked the prince quickly.

The king shook his head. "It's nothing I've learned. But there is a wild and monstrous suspicion growing within me, Lakki. But it's the only way I have found of answering the two questions I told you about. However, if my suspicions are anywhere like the truth, it is imperative we ask for the one thing that the Challoni would not be prepared to give us. I have a half formed, unsubstantiated guess about what it is. According to my estimate, we have about two hours left of the time Selzi gave us. At first I thought I would ask for more time. But I am fairly sure now that such a request will not be entertained. Selzi knows that I suspect something. This may possibly be the last . . . ."

CHAPTER 35

THE KING MAKES HIS CHOICE

The king broke off as the door of their little room opened. Selzi stood there. It held a covered tray which it wordlessly carried into the room and placed on the floor. "I have brought your food. I hope you have been able to give sufficient thought to the matter of what you want from us", it said. "In another hour I will call for you. We will be meeting the others and you can tell us then what you would like to take back to Earth with you". It looked at both of them expressionlessly and departed. The prince looked at his brother and nodded thoughtfully.

Thus it was that an hour later they found themselves again at the place where they had met the Challoni earlier. They were all there again. After they had settled down, Selzi looked at the prince. "We would like to hear you, first", it said. The prince looked around at the seated company. "You have been kind enough to take me around your city and show me many marvellous things there. Of all the things I saw, I thought nothing more marvellous than the fire throwing tubes of yours. I hope you will allow me to take some of those back to Earth". As the prince concluded, there was silence. Selzi then looked at him. "You can take as many of those as you can carry away", it said. There was another silence now.

The king started speaking slowly. "I, like my brother, have been amazed by the wonders of your city. Further, you have been very generous to us with the offer you have made". He stopped to look at the Challoni. "It is, in fact, such a generous offer that I wonder whether it would be fair to you to take its terms literally". He paused again. Selzi spoke now. "I . . . We . . . . I mean, I stand by whatever we have promised you. There is no question of going back on anything I have committed ourselves to. You can certainly tell us what it is you desire".

The king bowed. "I thank you. I need some help now. Can you wait here for some time till I can make some necessary preparations?" The Challoni seemed to be looking into the far distance. There was no reply. The weirdness struck the prince now as he remembered what his brother had told him. But the king seemed to think it the most natural thing in the world to wait patiently with nobody talking. Presently Selzi turned to the king. "We will wait here for you", it said.

The king got up now. "Lakki", he said, "come with me. I need your help". Prince Lakkan Pal walked in wondering silence behind his elder brother who seemed too preoccupied to talk. They reached the hall with the instruments now. The king went around, looking carefully at the various apparatuses there. He chose some of these with great care and kept them apart on a small table to the side. Presently he seemed satisfied with the choice of instruments and the two brothers started carrying them back, along with the table.

When they reached the place of the assembly, the table was placed on the ground. The king now busied himself with assembling the various pieces he had brought. He looked frowningly at the ensemble he had constructed and then hurried away. The prince guessed now that there was something else—some other part that was necessary for whatever he was putting together—that he must have missed and was going back to get. He returned in a few minutes with another piece and fitted it carefully into the instrument that was taking shape. The prince, who by this time was completely mystified about the object of this exercise, had given up any attempt to understand what was going on. He looked at the Challoni now. The group was sitting motionless and the prince noted that only Selzi was looking at the king as he moved about in rapt concentration on his task.

An hour must have gone by and the prince was awaiting the outcome of his brother's labours with an impatience that was growing steadily. Finally the king straightened and looked at the Challoni. "Can you come here, please? I have something to show you". He was addressing Selzi now. The prince thought that the older man was pointing to the apparatus he had put together and it crossed his mind that his elder brother, besotted with his Nalanda learning, had decided to ask for something that would further his esoteric studies. There was a flash of annoyance that rose now above the unquestioning faith he had for the king. The creature now got up, waddled towards the apparatus. The king knelt by it now and asked Selzi to do likewise. The creature carefully knelt down and seemed to be examining with extreme attention the assembly of discs and tubes.

But it could hardly have spent half a minute before it got up and went back to its position and sat down. The customary ceremony of silence ensued now and nobody spoke for some minutes. At the end of it, Selzi looked at the king. "King of Vithalla, you have chosen wisely. You have asked the one thing we had hoped you would not ask from us. But as we . . . I . . . have already said, I stand by my word to you. It is yours". After a short pause Selzi added: "Please be ready. You will be taken back to Earth immediately".

"You have given me everything I could hope for. Can I ask for just one more thing from you?" asked the king. "Certainly", Selzi replied. The king now pointed to the apparatus he had fabricated with such care. "I would like to take back these with me, if that is possible", he said. "It is yours", repeated Selzi without hesitation.

The king bowed. "In your generosity and your steadfastness in honouring your word, you have certainly shown yourself to be superior to the human species. I wish your species all fortune in finding soon a habitat more suitable than our planet", said the king.

CHAPTER 36

THE MAN WHO WON THE EARTH

It was some time later that the two men found themselves once again in the glade. It was night now. Two of the Challoni, after escorting them there, had melted away into the night. Moonlight was streaming into the little clearing now as the two men sat down with the burden they carried. They realized that they must have been gone for a little more than two days.

The prince looked at his brother. "Will you tell me one thing first, *Bhaiyya?* Why is it that you had to ask for those instruments when Selzi had already granted them to you?"

There was a puzzled look on the king's face as he asked: "But I asked for it only once".

It was the prince's turn to stare. "But after you had put those pieces together, didn't you show it to Selzi, ask him to look it, and then ask for it yourself?"

The king laughed. "I did not invite Selzi to look *at* the instruments, Lakki, but *through* them. But, since it immediately knew what it was that I was asking for, it did not need to look". There was blank incomprehension on the prince's face now. "I will tell you the story from the beginning, Lakki. But before that I will have to sleep first. I have not slept properly for two days now. I think it will be dawn in three hours. We will start then for home and I will tell you everything on the way".

"But, *Bhaiyya*", began the prince.

"Hush, Lakki", came the reply. "How many times have I told you that you shouldn't argue with your king". With that the king stretched himself out on the carpet of soft young grass and was immediately sound asleep.

"I made the cardinal mistake of trying to understand the Unknown through the Known, Lakki. It's a classic error. But that is no excuse. Thus, for example, when the Challoni promised us anything that we could *set eyes on,* and that it was *in their power to give*, almost till the last, I could not think beyond something that we were shown by the Challoni themselves—which is precisely what they wanted us to assume". The day had just dawned as the brothers started going down the mountain to the road that would lead to the city and the palace. "To take an even simpler instance of the same error, when confronted with the Challoni, I assumed that they would be like us, though I recognized they were not of the Earth", continued the king. "The first intimation that came to me that upset my pre-conceived notions was when I observed their communication with each other".

The king turned to look at the younger man. "Do you remember the scene of the fire? At that time my mind suddenly started receiving images of one of their species trapped in the space vehicle and being roasted to death. Thinking back on that, I realized that they could project images on human minds. But I forgot entirely about that when they started *speaking* to me. And they never penetrated my mind again. One reason for this was probably that in the urgency of that situation they could not afford to make the effort at normal speech. A second, I suspect, is that they did not want me to know they had the power of projecting mental images. If they could establish a mind-to-mind contact with a human, I could have realised that that would be their preferred method of communicating *between themselves*. Again when we were taken to their city, I got fresh evidence of it. You must have noticed the habit the Challoni had of lapsing suddenly into silence".

The prince slapped his forehead. "You mean they were mentally communicating with each other?"

"I'm almost sure of that, Lakki. But interesting as that was, it's implications are momentous. In fact, since it would betray a lot about their species, the Challoni, barring one occasion, tried their best to pretend their mode of communication was no different from ours, by affecting 'speech', in our presence. On the other hand, imagine, if you can, what happens to a species whose members can penetrate each other's minds. We can take refuge within our minds and none can follow us to that sanctuary, Lakki. But suppose that becomes possible, what happens then?" The king seemed to be talking to himself now and his companion felt no necessity to reply.

"The members of such a species lose their *sense of individuality*. And when self-referral becomes necessary for a member of such a species, it would be hopelessly lost in the choice between the 'I' word of individuality and the 'we' that denotes collectivity. Did you observe how confused Selzi used to get when it had to refer to itself? It could never seem to decide between 'I' and 'We'?"

There was a meditative pause now. "But I wish to go beyond even that. However, where I have been reasonably certain about what I have been saying till now, I must confess that what I will be claiming now must be a matter of conjecture—particularly since I believe no human being is ever going to set eyes on the Challoni again".

The king put down the load he had been carrying and massaged his arm. The prince now effortlessly picked it up and slung it over his own mighty shoulder. "You should let me do this, *Bhaiyya*. Now go on with your story".

"A story, it is, Lakki. But one which I hope is not too far from the truth. What I was going to say was, that it would be entirely possible for such a species as the Challoni to exist *as a single organism*, with what we perceive as individual members to *be merely the counterparts of various human limbs*. Granting this hypothesis, if I am allowed to pile one guess upon another, could it be possible that *the organism itself—or a large part of it, anyway—gets killed when one of its members dies?* Again, note how well the possibility accords with the rest of the facts. We have seen, first, the absence of any hierarchy among the Challoni. There doesn't even appear to be a leader among them. Also, remember that when Selzi was talking, it said that '*all of us*' are grateful to you for 'saving *our life*'. Even with the ambiguity of the Challoni's attempt with all self-reference, there seems to be more than an indication here of a single organism. One final piece of evidence is your own observation that their generosity seems excessive when you consider everything they were offering for saving *just one member of their species*".

"All these things amaze me. But they seem to fit into a pattern", said the prince.

"I cannot think of any other explanation which does, Lakki. So, it was their *species*, or at least a large part of it, that we saved". The king paused again. "And do you know what they were offering us as a reward?" The prince, looking at him intently, waited for his brother to continue. "They returned our world to us, Lakki", said the king quietly.

"But I'm getting ahead of my own story", said the king nodding to himself slowly. "When we reached the place, as I have already said, there were two questions that were bothering me. Why was it necessary to take us there and why at that particular time? Then I saw the instruments in the hall. It took some time for the truth to dawn, but I realised finally that they were *astronomical* instruments and, in fact, that the hall was an observatory. It was at this point that a tremendous piece of luck came to my aid. I had been an avid student of astronomy in Nalanda and I was familiar with some of the techniques for observing celestial bodies and recognised the functional aspects of some of these machines, at least. But do you know something, Lakki?" The king smiled at his brother. "It had never occurred to me that I would be putting the skills I had acquired there, to use instruments to *look at the Earth*".

"Look at the Earth?" asked the prince in astonishment. "Is that what you were doing?"

The king nodded. "When I saw the astronomical instruments displayed there, I knew there must have been some purpose behind it. When I started thinking about it, it suddenly occurred to me why we had been taken there. The reason was to take us far enough away from the Earth, Lakki. Since we had saved their entire species, the Challoni had decided to give us an opportunity to save ours. But they were not going to just give it away. If I wanted it, I would have to earn it. And so they—or should I say it?—devised a test for me".

The prince's eyes widened. "You put together that instrument so you could look at the Earth through it?" The king nodded. "And that was what Selzi found when it looked through it?"

The king shook his head. "No. Selzi did not need to look through it to know what I was indicating. *It knew*". The king told the other about how he had been surprised while examining the instruments. "When I came back to our room after realising what the instruments were, I suddenly saw how both my questions could be answered. We were brought here so that we could not ask for the world we stood on. It had to be far enough for the test to be a significant one. And the time too. The timing had to be perfect; for, I suspect that in a couple of days, if not hours, the motion of the world to which we have been transported, would have carried it to a position from which the Earth would not have been visible. You see, the Challoni were completely fair".

He paused now. "In fact, this fairness has marked their interaction, little as it has been, with the human species. I'll relate another instance of it and you can judge for yourself. Do you know when we first became aware of their presence?"

"During our grandfather's time?" asked the prince and the king nodded.

"The king, our grandfather, had a golden icon made and left it in the clearing for them. They took it, but a month later, they left in the clearing a gift for the king. It was a golden device, Lakki, wonderfully wrought, with, I'm sure, the gold from the icon. When placed in the sunlight, it drew power from it by some mysterious means and set spinning a golden orb to which were attached rods, with golden beads hanging from strings at their ends. It was commonly thought to be a cradle ornament for the king's infant son and was hung above the prince's cradle. But when the infant died a few days later, the king took it as an augury of evil and had it put away. How much of all this do you know, Lakki?"

"Well, I've heard that story from the palace servants, though nobody seems to know what happened to it. Most seem to believe, however, that the king secretly returned it to the glade, from where the Mountain Spirits took it back".

The king shook his head. "That is not true, Lakki. It passed into the hands of Tara Chand who, I think, from the beginning suspected that it was not a toy and the purpose behind it was much deeper than what it was commonly taken for. I think, before his death, he finally guessed what it was. Before his death, he left it to me in his will. Do you know what that golden bauble was, Lakki?" They had stopped now and the prince was staring at the king, hanging upon every word of his.

"It was a model—a model of the solar system, the Sun and his planetary family. And there are planets represented there *which we have not yet set eyes on, Lakki.*" They started walking again in silence for a few minutes, till presently the king resumed. "The motive behind the gift of the device could possibly have been twofold. One was certainly to announce the state of their knowledge and possibly even their extra terrestrial origins. But certain parts of that wonderful device I have not been able to understand yet. Maybe, when I understand it completely, I would find they had given clear intimation of where they come from and what their design was behind their presence on Earth.

A second intent could have been to test our reaction to it. Would we have the knowledge to understand the significance of what we had been given? If so, would we give some sign that we have understood? Again, it may also have been for a reason that has entirely escaped me." The king fell silent again. "When I think of the Challoni, I feel tempted to call them a morally sentient species, though as I have already occasion to remark, there are perils in trying to understand something alien to human nature in purely human terms".

There was a frown of puzzlement on the younger man's brow. "But when you asked for the Earth, you should know you couldn't have got it from the Challoni. But what do you mean by asking for it, anyway—or for that matter, what did the Challoni mean by giving it to you?"

"Simply this, Lakki. By asking for the world, I was asking them to withdraw from the world and return it to the human species; and on their part, by 'giving' me the world, they were acceding to my request and agreeing to renounce their claim on it. That is where we come to the most incredible part of the story, Lakki. The question we should have asked ourselves, but failed to. Why were the Challoni here? And how many of them were there and in what regions? We knew nothing about these things. Nor were we in any position to answer any of these questions.

Some day the world may be so connected that it may well become impossible for a species like the Challoni to land on one corner of it, however remote, without the news being instantly flashed over a global community. In that world, the Challoni may not have succeeded in any design of terrestrial occupation that did not involve an outright invasion. But what formidable weapons that world might be able to deploy in its defence cannot even be guessed at by us. But now we have no means of knowing even how many places in the world the Challoni have colonised.

And, in any case, in our unwisdom, the human community is capable of generating so much strife within itself that it has no time to attend to any external threats. A lesser instance of this observation is provided in the incident of Vichint's planned invasion. It gave us no time to examine what the motives of the Challoni could be. But if we come to think of it, it's a disturbing question. Why should a species which has acquired immense powers through a technology so advanced that we cannot even begin to understand it, arrive on Earth? Why, Lakki, what other intentions could they have except hostile ones, when they take every precaution to ensure that their presence is not detected?"

"If that is so, what were they waiting for?"

"I did ask myself that question. My answer would again have to be a guess. I have a feeling that they come from a world which is much farther away from the one to which we were taken. One indication is the fact that they did not appear to be able to move comfortably in that world. Another was the fact that there are too few of them there to have built a city like that. In all probability, it was just a transit station awaiting materials that would become necessary for a full scale invasion. So that, even with their tremendous powers, they may have felt that the time was not ripe to strike. But though they were not present here in sufficient numerical strength, they had started studying our manners and customs and could even speak our language. It might have been merely a matter of moving enough of their numbers into the Earth before they struck. Or maybe there was some other reason why they were not quite ready yet. But it was a matter of time, Lakki. And with their ability to penetrate human minds, they would have had designs on the Earth. After all, it would hardly serve their purpose to establish dominance over a small province of it, if they were to be surrounded by a human species resolved on expelling them". The king paused before continuing. "But all this is, at best, conjecture. While I feel that their ultimate object was to subjugate the human species or reduce it to serfdom, I'm much less sure about how they expected to encompass their aim. Anyway, by granting me my boon, they tacitly acknowledged that it was within their power to give me the Earth. They must have realised when I asked for the Earth, that I knew what their purpose on Earth was".

CHAPTER 37

THE PASSING OF RAM PAL

They had reached the road by this time and found the chariot waiting for them. As it began to roll along the road to the city, the king began speaking again. "I don't think it will be necessary any longer to bother ourselves with all that. When Selzi granted me my wish, it was not a mere agreement between the two of us, but a covenant between two species; and I know the Challoni will stand by their word and abide by the terms of that covenant and nobody is going to see them again".

The king stopped speaking. It was quite a while before he spoke again, and when he did so, it was in a musingly meditative vein, one almost of reverie. "I have a feeling in my bones, Lakki, that there is a shadow that has lifted from this kingdom. In the foreseeable future I do not expect any major crisis like those we have survived in the last year. It will be too much to expect, of course, that a whimsical Nature will not visit upon us the kind of calamities that have harassed us in the past. But I think, in a modest way, we have taken the first step to ensure that human folly will not add to those calamities. When I leave, it will be with the satisfaction of the knowledge that I have done what was in my power to give the people of Vithalla a king more worthy of that name and one upon whom kingship will sit with greater grace and majesty, and a statute that shall be responsive to their collective will. And having done that, I can consider my responsibilities at an end and the word I gave to my teacher to have been redeemed. I can then return in peace, Lakki, to the sphere to which I belong."

The king's words were to be prophetic. The year that followed was free from the kind of tumult that had marked the year that had gone before it. It was a period of quiet consolidation. On the domestic front, the establishment of the social institutions that the king had initiated, proceeded apace, while the kingdoms in the valley came together under a federation that promised to be strong enough to discourage external aggression. It was also an year in which the king progressively detached himself from the responsibilities of governance and began to spend more and more time with the instruments he had got from the Challoni.

One day the proclamation was made that the king would be abdicating the throne in favour of his younger brother, prince Lakkan Pal. Rumour began its whispering work then. Prince Lakkan Pal's harsh criticism of the king in front of his own council was public knowledge and there were those who said that the king had chosen this way of registering his displeasure. There would be a 'reconciliation', they argued. The prince would be made to abase himself for his arrogance and that would be the end of the matter. There were others who argued that it was a palace coup. The queen had a powerful coterie behind her who wanted to see the prince enthroned.

The head priest, however, when somebody discreetly questioned him, scorned to countenance the tattle of the tongue wagging ignorants. Nobody had realized what had happened, he said, broadly intimating by cryptic hints, that he had. Upon being wheedled and coaxed, he had finally let it be known—after binding his listeners to a solemn oath of secrecy whose violation would involve the penalty of a long and lingering death—that it was the old king's doing. He had extracted a promise from his elder son that after he had ruled over the kingdom for a specified period, he was to hand over the kingship to his younger brother.

"But why did he do it?" queried one of his shocked audience.

"Why?" echoed the priest and looked at the questioner in pitying contempt. "Think for yourself", he answered mysteriously and firmly declined to go any further into a secret that concerned the royal household.

Some of the rumours reached the king. Whether it was this that decided him or whether the old longing had returned with a force whose insistent clamour could no longer be denied, the king, after consulting the astrologer, set an auspicious date for the transfer of power. Thus it was that before the people could completely get over their surprise, the coronation of the prince had taken place. But whatever the initial response of the people had been, it was with satisfaction that the king learned that the measure found broad approval.

A few days after this, the new king and his brother were again at the glade. From where they stood, they could look down on their kingdom. They had been standing there for some time, absorbed in that peace of that scene, when the older man spoke. "There is one last responsibility that remains for me, Lakki", he said. The other looked at him. "For that, I have a request to make of you".

The young king looked at him in wide eyed wonder at that. "You know you do not have to request me for anything. There is nothing I have which you have not bestowed on me". The other was silent for a long minute. "However, I do not know how much right I have to make this request, since this pertains to your own personal life. But since you have bid me speak, I will go on. The queen and I feel that you must soon choose a young woman to sit as queen by your side. Have you given the matter any thought?"

The young man looked at him thoughtfully. "I have left the matter to you", he said.

"I gather, then, that you have no particular person in mind. If that is so, I would like to make a suggestion. Have you seen Tham's sister?"

"Mithilesh?" asked the other quickly, in some surprise.

The other nodded. "That's not her name, of course. When she was studying with me at Nalanda, her foreign sounding name did not come easily to us". He smiled. "Mithilesh was as close as we could get to it".

"But . . . . She's not even of this country", said the king with a wondering frown.

There was a pause before the other spoke. "I do not think that will matter very much", he said finally. He continued: "She has intelligence and spirit, Lakki. You will find those traits to be inestimable assets in a woman who will sit on the throne by your side. While I do not say she doesn't have her share of human imperfections, her genuine strengths are more precious than a descent from a line of kings, or the dowry that she would bring. Besides, there is another matter". He stopped.

"Yes", prompted the king.

"To be a king, Lakki, is to be willing to relinquish a large part of your rights as an individual. We have decided already that, in time, Tham is going to be your chief minister". The older man paused again as, in his mind's eye a vision arose of his young associate from Nalanda. Tham had shown an unsuspected side of his character in the gifts he had displayed of his shrewdness and his capability in handling men. But would he have unsuspected depths of ambition, too? There was another image that arose in his mind now, of the young king of Vithalla, trusting and impetuous. He continued now. "I'm sure you realise the obvious advantages that will ensue in strengthening that relationship by one of marriage". The king looked at his elder brother in some surprise. "I have taken the liberty of discussing this matter with the queen, our mother. I am happy to say that the few initial reservations she had about such an unusual alliance were laid to rest when I explained the benefits of having Mithilesh as your queen".

The silence that fell this time lasted longer. Finally the king turned to his elder brother. "It shall be as you wish, *bhaiyya*", he said.

Shortly after this, the proclamation was made that Vithalla was to have a new queen. After their wedding, king Lakkan Pal and queen Mithilesh were taken in a chariot round the city, with the former king himself acting as the charioteer. He had intended the gesture as a farewell to his people, having decided this was the last time they would see him.

An year after this, it was summer and a brilliant moon hung high in the sky. Late on that night, a chariot rolled out of the palace and through the streets of a sleeping city. It carried the former king of Vithalla—Ram Pal as he would want to be called now. Earlier, in a brief ceremony at the palace, he had taken leave of his mother, his younger brother and a few close associates. He had insisted that, as private citizen, his passing from the palace should attract no more attention than that. The chariot now left him at the edge of the forest, where a footpath ran up to the mountains.

Ram Pal walked steadily, a small bundle of his personal possessions hardly costing him any effort to carry. In a few hours he had reached the glade. He sat down then to look at the valley below. The peace of that scene was to stay a long time with him. He thought then of all the times he had come to that glade and of all the climactic incidents of his life that had taken place there and indeed of all the momentous events there that had materially affected the destiny of his country even before he had been born.

He had already lived for a longer time than the human span that was normal in that age and clime and knew that it was exceedingly unlikely that he would ever see the valley again. He must have sat there longer than he had intended, for he saw now the reddening east that signalled the dawn. He got up then, turned his back on his throne, his kingdom, his people and the world he had won and with a light heart, set his face towards the long road that would lead to Nalanda.

*   *   *

A small breeze had sprung up now as the story ended. Several of those who had come to hear the story were now asleep, their blankets drawn around them against the cold. Tulsi looked around at the assembly and presently his attention came to rest on the figure of Sukh Ram. "Would you like to own as much land as the king of Vithalla, Sukh Ram?" he asked. The man he addressed was, however, fast asleep, his head sunk on his breast, like a barn sparrow. Tulsi now rose, took the lamp and disappeared into the temple with it. This was the signal for the congregation to start getting up.

Prasad stole a look at his companion. Steinhardt was sitting still, like a figure carved out of stone.

Overhead, the moon blazed with silver fire.

GLOSSARY

PROLOGUE

In one of the most ancient of Hindu scriptures, the *Bhagavata Purana*, the story is told of king Bali, who was mighty enough to conquer the *Devaloka*, or the kingdom of the lesser gods. The *Devas*, the inhabitants of the kingdom, thereupon threw themselves on the mercy of Vishnu, one of the supreme trinity of the Hindu pantheon, to recover their lost realm. Vishnu, loth to do battle with a noble and just king like Bali, resolved instead, to resort to strategem. He took the guise of a young Brahmin boy called Vamana and attended the *yagna* or the great religious ceremony conducted by Bali to honour God.

Upon these occasions, it was obligatory for the performer of the *yagna* to grant whatever was asked of him to any who had attended the ceremony. Vamana now approached king Bali and requested as much land as three of his steps could enclose. The king, ignorant of the identity of the visitor, immediately granted this modest boon.

Whereupon, Vamana immediately assumed cosmic dimensions. With his first step, he took in all of Earth and with his second, all heaven. He then turned to the king and asked him where he could he could put his foot down for his third step. King Bali, realising the ruse that had been played upon him by none less than the lord, was nevertheless, magnanimous enough to stand by the word he had given and now humbly bowed down and offered his own head, in token of his submission, for Vishnu to put his foot upon. Whereupon, Vishnu, realising the nobility of the king, pardoned him and bestowed immortality upon him.

p5 ji: A semi-formal term of address.

p7 Ramayan: One of the two major Hindu epics, the other being Mahabharat

p7 Chandigarh: The city is situated 250 kms North of Delhi

p4 Lahaul-Spiti: This is a district in present day Himachal Pradesh of India. It comprises of the two regions of Lahaul and Spiti.

p14 Tulsi Ata: This is an anagram of 'Tusitala'—meaning 'storyteller'—in the language of the natives of Tahiti, among whom Robert Louis Stevenson spent his last days.

p13 The ruins of Troy: Steinhardt's reference here is to the archaeological discoveries of Henry Schliemann.

p17 Shimla: The city of Shimla is the capital of the state of Himachal Pradesh.

p25 Saraswathi: In the Rig Veda, accorded by some the status of the oldest extant literature of the world, there are references to the river Saraswathi. In Sanskrit, the name means "river with many pools".

There is some dispute over the location of the river, from its references in mythology. One group of scholarly opinion, Max Muller's among them, seek to locate it in the Ghaggar valley, while others claim for it locations varying from Afghanistan to the Rann of Kutch, in Gujarat.

p75, 80 Nalanda: Nalanda was one of the oldest centres of higher learning of the ancient world. Flourishing roughly from the 5th century to the 12th century AD, it was located in the present day state of Bihar in India. It was supported by Hindu and Buddhist kings alike—like the Guptas and Harsha. In its heyday, it attracted scholars and students from Tibet, China, Greece and Persia. The entire university complex stood on fourteen hectares.

In the year 1193, Nalanda was ransacked and destroyed by the army of king Bhaktiar Khilji. It has been said that the huge library of Nalanda kept burning for three months after it was set fire to. Recently, in 2006, under the initiative and funding of Singapore, China, India and Japan, a plan has been drawn up for the establishment of an international university at Nalanda.

p120 Bhaiyya: "Brother". A term of respectful familiarity, such as may be used to address an elder brother.

p131 Bhim: There are two great Hindu epics—The Ramayan and the Mahabharat. The latter describes the great internecine war between the two clans of the *Kauravas* and the *Pandavas*. Bhim is the second of the five brothers who constitute the *Pandava* clan. A giant in stature, he is known for his tremendous physical strength.

p150, 151 Krishna: The central character of the Mahabharat. He is called the 'Sutradhar' of the epic—in Sanskrit, the moving spirit under which everything that happens in Mahabharat takes place. He is the physical incarnation of Vishnu and one his greatest and best known avatars. Kishan Dev slyly reminds Vichint that the lowly born and slight statured Krishna (compared here to king Ram Pal) was an infinitely greater force than the great Bhim himself (from whom Vichint claims descent).

p75 Prince Siddhartha: He was later to be known as the Buddha

P151 Metaphysical discourse: This was the Bhagavad Gita

ACKNOWLEDGEMENTS

It is a pleasure to thank Akshay. The assistance he rendered was invaluable and its instances too numerous to be mentioned here.